P9-DHP-135

IT WAS IMPOSSIBLE TO MARRY SUCH AN IMPOSSIBLE MAN

Frances Stewart had managed to do the sensible thing once when she rejected the impetuous courtship of Ian Macdonald and wed the English lord who offered her the best of all possible marriages.

But Frances was a young widow now, and Ian was home from the wars, as infuriating and as irresistible as ever.

It would be sheer folly for Frances to yield to this man whom she had so wisely evaded once. It would be even more unthinkable to make him the official father of the young daughter who the world did not suspect was really his.

Frances once again had the chance to do the sensible thing— but she also had to deal with that madness called love. . . .

The Scottish Lord

More Regency Romances from SIGNET

☐ **THE DETERMINED BACHELOR** by Judith Harkness.
(#J9609—$1.95)

☐ **THE MONTAGUE SCANDAL** by Judith Harkness.
(#E8922—$1.75)*

☐ **THE ADMIRAL'S DAUGHTER** by Judith Harkness.
(#E9161—$1.75)*

☐ **A LONDON SEASON** by Joan Wolf.   (#J9570—$1.95)

☐ **A KIND OF HONOR** by Joan Wolf.   (#E9296—$1.75)*

☐ **THE COUNTERFEIT MARRIAGE** by Joan Wolf.
(#E9064—$1.75)*

☐ **LORD HARRY'S FOLLY** by Catherine Coulter.
(#E9531—$1.75)*

☐ **LORD DEVERILL'S HEIR** by Catherine Coulter.
(#E9200—$1.75)*

☐ **THE REBEL BRIDE** by Catherine Coulter.   (#J9630—$1.95)

☐ **THE AUTUMN COUNTESS** by Catherine Coulter.
(#E8463—$1.75)*

☐ **AMELIA** by Megan Daniel.   (#E9487—$1.75)*

☐ **THE INCOMPARABLE MISS BRADY** by Sheila Walsh.
(#E9245—$1.75)*

☐ **MADELENA** by Sheila Walsh.   (#E9332—$1.75)

☐ **LORD GILMORE'S BRIDE** by Sheila Walsh.   (#E8600—$1.75)*

☐ **THE GOLDEN SONGBIRD** by Sheila Walsh.   (#E8155—$1.75)†

☐ **THE SERGEANT MAJOR'S DAUGHTER** by Sheila Walsh.
(#E8220—$1.75)

*Price slightly higher in Canada
†Not available in Canada

Buy them at your local bookstore or use this convenient coupon for ordering.

THE NEW AMERICAN LIBRARY, INC.,
P.O. Box 999, Bergenfield, New Jersey 07621

Please send me the books I have checked above. I am enclosing $_____
(please add $1.00 to this order to cover postage and handling). Send check
or money order—no cash or C.O.D.'s. Prices and numbers are subject to change
without notice.

Name_____

Address_____

City _____ State _____ Zip Code _____
Allow 4-6 weeks for delivery.
This offer is subject to withdrawal without notice.

The Scottish Lord

by Joan Wolf

A SIGNET BOOK
NEW AMERICAN LIBRARY
TIMES MIRROR

PUBLISHER'S NOTE

This novel is a work of fiction. Names, characters, places, and incidents are either the product of the author's imagination or are used fictitiously, and any resemblance to actual persons, living or dead, events, or locales is entirely coincidental.

NAL BOOKS ARE AVAILABLE AT QUANTITY DISCOUNTS WHEN USED TO PROMOTE PRODUCTS OR SERVICES. FOR INFORMATION PLEASE WRITE TO PREMIUM MARKETING DIVISION, THE NEW AMERICAN LIBRARY, INC., 1633 BROADWAY, NEW YORK, NEW YORK 10019.

Copyright © 1981 by Joan Wolf

All rights reserved

SIGNET TRADEMARK REG. U.S. PAT. OFF. AND FOREIGN COUNTRIES
REGISTERED TRADEMARK—MARCA REGISTRADA
HECHO EN CHICAGO, U.S.A.

SIGNET, SIGNET CLASSICS, MENTOR, PLUME, MERIDIAN and NAL BOOKS are published by The New American Library, Inc., 1633 Broadway, New York, New York 10019

First Printing, January, 1982

1 2 3 4 5 6 7 8 9

PRINTED IN THE UNITED STATES OF AMERICA

Chapter One

She's bonnie, blooming, straight, and tall,
And lang has had my heart in thrall
—ROBERT BURNS

"If you will step into the drawing room, Mr. Macdonald," the butler said, giving Douglas the distinct impression that a very great favor was about to be conferred upon him, "Miss Stewart will be down directly."

Douglas nodded gravely and allowed himself to be conducted into the proper room. The butler withdrew and Douglas moved toward the pictures as though drawn by a magnet. He was examining them carefully when the door opened and Frances Stewart came into the room. She stood for a moment in silence, regarding the absorbed figure before her.

Douglas Macdonald was a pleasant-looking man of twenty-six. His medium brown hair was neatly cut and brushed and his clothing was well tailored and fashionable, but there was something ineffably unsettled about him. Frances smiled tolerantly. She knew the look well. Her father was a famous classics scholar and he often wore the same air. It was the aura of a man whose mind is on other things. "Hello, Douglas," she said, amusement sounding in the rich contralto tones of her voice.

He turned immediately. "Frances! How good to see you." She came toward him and reached up to kiss his cheek, saying something in response to his greeting. For a long moment he did not reply.

All her life Frances Stewart would have that effect upon people. Her face combined exquisite coloring with a hauntingly perfect bone structure that, Douglas had once told her, would keep her beautiful until she was eighty. He said now, in total disregard of her gracious welcome, "I wish you'd let me paint you."

She looked surprised. "I didn't think you did people."

"I don't, usually, but I'd like to do you."

"All right," she said agreeably. "Please sit down, Douglas. Aunt Mary is out, I'm afraid, and she will doubtless read me a lecture on the propriety of entertaining gentlemen in her absence, but I'm glad to have you to myself. It's been so long! What have you been doing with yourself?"

He sat down on a delicate-looking sofa and watched her calmly. "I've just come from Edinburgh," he said.

"Oh." The curves of her lips thinned. "Then I gather you've seen Ian."

"Briefly. He went to Castle Hunter for a few weeks, but came back to Edinburgh. He had a row with his mother, I'm afraid."

Her eyes flashed. The brilliant color of them had always been surprising. "He seems to be having rows with everyone these days. He couldn't quarrel with me in person because I left Edinburgh before he got there, but he had the colossal cheek to send me a letter asking me what I was doing wasting my time making a London come-out. What does he expect me to do, for heaven's sake?''

"Wait for him, I imagine," he answered imperturbably.

She jumped to her feet and paced about the room, long-legged and graceful. "I have better things to do than wait for Ian to grow up," she said over her shoulder to his quiet figure.

There was a pause while he digested this startling statement. "You know he's been sent down from Cambridge, I take it." He spoke cautiously.

"Oh, yes." She subsided into a chair. At eighteen there was still something faintly boyish about Frances. It came, Douglas thought, from all those years of running free with Ian. It only added to her quite considerable charm. "Do you know what he was expelled for, Douglas?" she demanded.

"I heard something about a rooftop race through the town," he admitted.

"They all ended up in the Cam. Stinking drunk." Disgustedly she pushed a stray curl off her face. "If it had been the first time they might have let him come back, but it wasn't. Even Charlie's intercession didn't help. He's out."

He was staring at her, faint surprise in his eyes. "Did Ian tell you all that?"

She lifted a faint, ironical eyebrow. "Hardly. I had it from Charlie."

"Oh."

"What's the matter with Ian, Douglas?" she asked with unsmiling intensity. "He was always wild, but getting thrown out of Cambridge is more than that. It affects his whole future."

"You used to be pretty wild yourself," he hedged. "Remember the time you and Ian impersonated the ghost of Glencoe and scared that poor Sassenach family all the way back to London?"

Frances grinned impishly, an expression so enchanting that Douglas ached to catch it on canvas. "That was one of our better efforts," she admitted. But she was not to be deterred. "This is different," she insisted. "He wanted to be thrown out of Cambridge. That's why he organized that silly race. And everyone followed him because . . . oh, because he's Ian and twice as alive as everyone else. People would follow him if he announced he were going to the moon!"

Douglas allowed his gaze to dwell upon her calmly. "You know why he got himself thrown out of Cambridge, Frances," he said evenly. "You don't need me to tell you. Ian would have told you himself, if you had given him the chance."

Her head was slightly bent. She was staring at the Persian carpet and the austerity of the set of her lips and the somberness of her eyes were startling on her usually serene face. "He wants to go to the Peninsula," she said flatly.

"Of course he does." Douglas's voice was very gentle.

"Ever since Alan was killed at Talavera and Lady Lochaber made him promise he would not join the army he has been like this." She raised her head and her eyes now were bright with anger. "I perfectly see Lady Lochaber's point. One son dead in Portugal is quite enough. I don't understand why Ian won't be satisfied until he too has a chance to be mowed down by a rain of bullets." She looked at Douglas, a shadow of anxiety

4

in her eyes. "That was what the row with his mother was about, I take it?"

"Yes."

"She hasn't given in?"

"No."

The shadow cleared. "Good for her, I say."

"I don't know, Frances," he said slowly. "Ian is ripe to do something reckless."

"He won't go to Portugal," she said positively. "It is not easy to pin Ian down to a promise, but once he gives his word he keeps it." She frowned, her fine eyebrows slanting slightly upward. "Why is he so set on joining the army, Douglas? It's become an obsession with him."

Douglas leaned back in his chair, his eyes level on her face. "Women never like it when their men want to go off to war," he commented neutrally.

She looked back at him thoughtfully, almost remotely. "He won't be mine if he goes to Portugal. I don't want a soldier for a husband."

His mouth was suddenly dry. She was deadly serious. "Have you told that to Ian?"

"Oh, yes." Her eyebrows were like fine aloof arches over her coolly distant eyes. "Obviously he didn't believe me. Or he didn't care. Otherwise he never would have gotten himself thrown out of Cambridge."

"Not care!" He stared at her incredulously. "You can't believe that."

"What else am I to believe?"

He looked at her sealed face and his mouth twisted in a wry smile. She was so young. How could she possibly understand the demons that drove a boy like Ian? Out of loyalty to his cousin he tried to explain. "Ian needs to be *doing* something, Frances," he said at last. "It is unfortunate he is not the eldest son; there is much in Lochaber that needs to be done. But he is not the earl and he won't meddle in what belongs to Charlie."

"He could become a lawyer. It is what he was going to do after he left Cambridge."

"It is what you and Lady Lochaber wanted him to do, not what Ian wanted. Frances, Ian needs a wider canvas to exercise his energy than the law would ever provide. In the Scotland of a hundred years ago there was scope for a man of his caliber. Today there is not." He smiled crookedly. "The times are out of joint for him, Frances."

Her face had hardened. "He would have made a good brigand, you mean."

He grinned. "He would have," he agreed.

Unwillingly she smiled back. "You've always defended him."

"I've never had to defend him to you before."

The smile faded. "I know." She straightened her slim shoulders. "Goodness, you've been here for half an hour and all we've done is talk about Ian! What about you, Douglas? What are you doing in London and how long do you plan to stay?"

"I've taken rooms in Jermyn Street," he replied. "I plan to take in some lectures at the Royal Academy. If I want to become established as an artist, London is the place to begin."

"I suppose so." She smiled at him warmly. "I hope you'll have time for some socializing. If I send you a card for Aunt Mary's ball next week will you come?"

It was a moment before he replied, but when he did

his voice was expressionless. "I should be happy to Is your father in London as well?"

"Papa?" There was another ironic lift of her eyebrows. "He is in Edinburgh, of course, immersed in his books. You didn't think he would dream of subjecting himself to the frivolity of a London season?"

Douglas had met Sir Donal Stewart on several occasions. He laughed. "No, I can't quite see him making idle conversation over a glass of champagne punch."

"He would more than likely deliver himself of a learned dissertation on the authorship of Homer, or some such topic. Papa does not have the knack of idle conversation."

"He'll talk about you."

"I'd rather he talked about Homer!" Frances shook her head. "Anyone who thinks they are getting a good reading of my character from Papa is in for a sad disappointment. He decided when I was born that I was perfect, and once Papa makes up his mind about someone nothing can change it. Probably because he scarcely notices anyone who inhabits his own time sphere. If I were Antigone, now, he would have a much more varied opinion about me."

There was some truth in what she said, but not as it pertained to her. Douglas had seen the light in Sir Donal's eyes when they rested on his only daughter. "I doubt it," he said merely.

He stayed for another ten minutes and then took his leave, having promised once again to attend Lady Mary Graham's ball. As he drove himself home to his lodgings in Jermyn Street his brow was furrowed. His conversation with Frances had disturbed him greatly.

When Ian had asked him to call on Frances and see

7

how she was doing he had been suspicious. Ian had never before needed an intermediary. Douglas understood the request now that he had seen Frances. Obviously she was furious with Ian.

It was serious. For one thing, Frances was rarely out of temper. There was a characteristic sweetness and serenity about her that Douglas had loved since first he met her six years ago. But that unruffled tranquility hid a temperament capable of great passion and a resolve that was formidable in one so young. It was easy to be soft and charming when your will was never thwarted. Douglas had seen Frances crossed once or twice; in a battle of wills she had always won.

There was only one other person Douglas knew who had a determination to match Frances's. The first move in the game had gone to her; obviously she had hastily accepted her aunt's repeated invitation to launch her into London society in order to punish Ian. She had left Edinburgh before he arrived. Just what she planned to do, however, remained unclear to Douglas. He decided to spend a few weeks observing her before writing to his cousin.

Chapter Two

O whistle, and I'll come to ye, my lad
—ROBERT BURNS

Frances had first gone to Castle Hunter, ancient seat of the Macdonalds of Lochaber, in the summer of her twelfth year. Her mother had been Lady Lochaber's best friend, both of them having in their girlhood been the only Scots and the only Catholics at a prestigious English seminary for young ladies. Frances's mother was Helen Graham, niece of the Duke of Montrose, and exquisitely lovely. When she had married Donal Stewart, a dreamy young scholar from Appin, her relatives had been disappointed. Helen, they universally felt, could have done better for herself.

Flora Cameron, on the other hand, had married Charles Macdonald, Earl of Lochaber. The Macdonalds had been chiefs of Glencoe and Lochaber since time out of mind. They had survived the notorious massacre perpetuated by the Campbells in 1692; they had survived the disastrous Rising of 1745 when they had fought for Charles Edward Stuart against the German king in London; they had survived the stigma of their religion which they stubbornly retained even though it kept the earl from taking his seat in the House of Lords. They owned virtually all of Lochaber and Glencoe, most of which land was leased to crofters who raised cattle for the Lowlands and England. They were not rich, but in the affairs of Scotland they were immensely powerful. It had been a good match for Flora Cameron.

She had been godmother to Helen's only child, Frances, and when news came to Castle Hunter that Helen had died, she invited the girl to spend the summer in Lochaber. Sir Donal, grief-stricken by his wife's sudden death, wanted only to get away from Edinburgh. He was going to Greece and not quite sure what to do with Frances. Flora Macdonald's invitation had been a godsend.

So Frances was sent to Lochaber. She had Highland blood in her and had responded instantly to the majestic beauty of Castle Hunter and its surroundings. The castle was old; it dated from the thirteenth century although it had been added to in succeeding generations. The main floor was chiefly occupied by the Great Hall, which had been built as a royal hunting seat in the thirteenth century. It was a mammoth room, with walls of stone and a floor of ancient tile. In the early days of its royal ownership it was used to feed and house a household of several hundred, but when the house passed to the Macdonalds in the fifteenth century the upper floors were the ones renovated and used by the family. By the time Frances came to Castle Hunter, the Great Hall was used mainly by the Macdonald children for indoor play on rainy days. The real living quarters were on the first and second floors. The rooms were not elaborate; the

Macdonalds had always been Jacobites and Catholics and consequently never had very much money, but their home was charming, with its seventeenth-century white paneling and comfortable, tasteful furniture.

The real beauty of Castle Hunter lay in its location. It stood on an island in the clear waters of Loch Leven, connected to the shore by a stone causeway. From the castle's small windows, which looked as if they had been burrowed through its thick stone walls, one could look out upon the towering heights of Ben Nevis and the wild mountains of Lochaber.

Douglas's memories of Frances were all connected with Castle Hunter. During the week that followed his visit to her in London, he found himself thinking a great deal about her. She was constantly in his mind, not so much as she was when he had seen her in her aunt's drawing room, but as he remembered her from the past.

He had been home from Cambridge when Frances first arrived at Castle Hunter. Douglas's father was Lord Lochaber's brother, and Douglas had come to stay with the Macdonalds when his father had gone off to India with Lord Cornwallis. His father had died, his mother had remarried, and Douglas had stayed on at the Castle. Lord Lochaber's death two years previously had made no difference to his status. Lady Lochaber regarded him as another son and had sent him off to Cambridge with Charlie and Alan.

The three of them were at Castle Hunter for the summer holiday the year of Frances's introduction into the Macdonald clan. She had been such a sweet child, Douglas remembered, gentle and tender and trusting. She was her parents' only one and clearly they had not suffered the winds to blow ungently upon her. Her mother's death had shaken her, but the deep security they had given to her had not been pierced.

And she was lovely. Douglas remembered vividly the feelings of tenderness and protectiveness the rosy-faced child who held her head like a flower on a stem had provoked in him. He had wanted to guard her, to walk before her to remove each little stone that she might have dashed her foot against. She had spent most of her time with him.

And then Ian came home from Eton. At fourteen he was tall, arrogant with adolescent superiority, and alight with the flame that made all those who stood beside him look only half alive. Frances had thought he was wonderful. To twelve the age of twenty is awesome, but fourteen is magnetic. Without a qualm Frances dropped Douglas and gravitated to Ian. He, not unflattered by her obvious adoration, had with casual possessiveness annexed her as his chief follower. They were always out, either on foot with the dogs, on the loch, or on horseback over the lovely, lonely hills.

Against Douglas's careful, tender guardianship she had chosen Ian. He was wild and reckless and had never guarded anything in his life. He plunged her into physical hardship and, often, physical danger. He bossed her and teased her. He regarded her as his.

The years had passed and every summer Frances had returned to Castle Hunter. Lady Lochaber was very fond of her and, since Frances was always beautifully polite, had allowed her to go her own way. Her own way had, invariably, been Ian's way. And Ian went uncurbed.

Douglas, whose feelings for Frances had only deepened with time, was an interested onlooker of her life.

The first real indication of a change in her relationship with Ian had come the summer she was sixteen. Ian, now eighteen, had been allowed to join the family in the main dining room when company was present, and Lady Lochaber had broken her own rule and had said Frances might come downstairs as well. The occasion had been Charlie's arrival with an English friend, Lord Henry Talbot, a young man the same age as Charlie, twenty-five.

For the first time Frances had worn her hair up. Lord Henry had not been able to take his eyes off her all during dinner. Charlie, who hadn't seen her in two years, was having the same trouble. Frances had not noticed. She conversed with meticulous courtesy with the gentlemen on either side of her, who happened to be Ian and Alan. Her cheeks had been flushed and her eyes bright with the pleasure of her first grown-up dinner party.

Ian had noticed the reaction of his brother and his guest. On one or two occasions he had caught their gaze and both had been startled by the expression in those dark eyes. When they joined the women in the drawing room Ian had gone directly to where Frances sat, stood behind her and, with lordly possessiveness, placed a hand on her shoulder. It was a picture that remained vividly in Douglas's mind, that image of Ian standing behind Frances with the firelight illuminating the thick fall of his dark hair and his dark, challenging eyes.

There was one other picture from that summer that Douglas remembered clearly. It had been the end of August. Frances and Ian had ridden out toward Glencoe earlier in the day when Sir Donal had unexpectedly arrived at Castle Hunter. Douglas had volunteered to

13

find Frances and let her know her father had come.

The pass of Glencoe was a haunted place. Douglas had always felt that the savage betrayal of the massacre, when a company of Campbell soldiers had put to the sword the Macdonald clan who had housed them with sacred Highland hospitality, had imprinted itself on the landscape. The precipitous rock faces that surround the pass reminded him of a savage army of gaunt peaks, scarred by bleak ravines. The place was heavy with brooding melancholy, even in the sunlight of a fair August day.

The girl and boy whom Douglas sought did not seem to be aware of any unpleasant atmosphere. They were standing near the great flat rock that heads the glen. Instinctively Douglas pulled his horse up. The picture they made, with the mountains of Beinn Fhada, Gearr Aonach, and Aonach Dubh as their backdrop, was stunning enough to cause him to want to capture it in memory. He watched them for a moment, with a painter's abstract eye.

As Douglas looked on Frances shook her head at something Ian was saying to her. In response he laughed and pulled at the ribbon that was tying back her hair. It gave, and the heavy shining mass of it swung loose. The girl snatched at the ribbon and as she turned toward him he caught her shoulders. Frances had grown quite tall, but she had to tip her head back to look up into Ian's face.

He said something to her and then, as Douglas watched helplessly, his mouth came down on hers and her head tilted back so that her hair fell in a curtain of pale gold over the arm that had pulled her hard against him. Her arms went up to circle his neck.

14

Douglas dug his heels into the sides of his horse and rode forward. They moved apart slowly at his approach. Frances's eyes were like emeralds. Ian's face looked both fierce and wary. He kept Frances's hand in his. In the end Douglas had not said anything, and they had returned together to the castle.

It was Alan's death the following year that had driven a rift between them. Frances had been at Castle Hunter when word came in early August that he had fallen in the Battle of Talavera. He was five years older than Ian and had joined the army when he left Cambridge. He had been in the Peninsula for only six months.

Lady Lochaber was distraught. The rest of the family sincerely mourned for Alan, but she seemed inconsolable. Ian loved his mother, and when she had begged him to promise her he would stay out of the army he had done so. It was a promise he almost instantly regretted.

Douglas had sympathized with him. All his life Ian had planned to join the army. As a younger son it was one of the few professions open to him. He was a Roman Catholic, so there was no family living waiting for him as there was for so many of the younger sons of the English nobility who belonged to the Church of England. His religion also barred him from representing his family constituency in the House of Commons. And while Ian was hardly a deeply religious person he would as soon have thought of changing his religion as changing the color of his hair. He was a Macdonald of Lochaber and the Macdonalds of Lochaber had always been Catholics. And so what was left for him was the army. Or the law.

For Ian it had always been the army. It was a profession for which Douglas had always thought he was well suited. He had the instant, unreflecting courage of all great soldiers, as well as the kind of personality that commanded instant admiration and respect, an invaluable quality in an officer. Furthermore, he was interested in international politics, and Douglas and he had talked for many hours about Britain's intervention in Spain. Ian was a Scot, a passionate believer in individual liberty and the rights of all nations to rule themselves as they chose. Napoleon's invasion of Spain was, to his mind, indefensible. Both he and Douglas had agreed that the freedom of Spain was well worth fighting for.

Only now he would not be fighting. A Cambridge career and the law were the only goals left for him. He did not find them attractive. And Douglas, watching sympathetically, saw another frustration arise for Ian. For the first time in five years, Frances was against him.

The problem with detachment, Douglas often reflected wryly, was that you tended to see all sides of an issue. He understood and empathized with Ian. He also saw Frances's point of view with compassionate comprehension.

Alan's death had jolted Frances profoundly. She was not deeply interested in causes or ideology, and her knowledge of what was happening in Spain and Portugal was extremely limited. She knew Ian was going to join the army, but she had not thought much beyond the vision of him dressed in regimentals and looking magnificent. He had been shrewd enough not to dwell upon his ardor for war in her presence.

But Alan was dead. Douglas would always remember her expression in the weeks that followed the message from the War Department. The childlike, trusting look he had loved was gone. In its place was a gray look of worry that had drained the youth from her face. The look had gone only after Lady Lochaber extracted that promise from Ian.

When Ian turned to Frances for understanding he got only a face of stone. The romantic haze had cleared from before her eyes and she saw the future in the cold, sunless light of reality. "You're no good to me dead on some battlefield in Portugal," she had said to him brutally within Douglas's hearing one day. "The law is a perfectly good profession. We can live quite comfortably on my money and on what you make." And, finally, out of her fear and out of her youth, she had given him an ultimatum. "I won't marry you if you become a soldier."

Now Ian had succeeded in getting himself thrown out of Cambridge. There would be no career in the law. He was determined, Douglas knew, to force his mother to release him from his promise. He had always been her favorite son. He was confident she would give in. And, knowing Ian, Douglas was also sure that he thought he could win Frances over. In the past she had always done what he wanted her to do. But Douglas, remembering that austere and somber look he had seen on her face, was very much afraid those days were over.

17

Chapter Three

To see her is to love her,
  And love but her for ever,
For nature made her what she is,
  And never made anither!

—ROBERT BURNS

The season of 1810 was remembered in the social history of London as the year Frances Stewart made her come-out. In succeeding years the story of the impact she made on the sophisticated London ton would assume proportions that were almost mythical. The reality was astounding enough, as Douglas Macdonald often thought when he heard it talked about in future years. He had been there and watched it all, the private drama as well as the public success.

It began at the ball given by her aunt, Lady Mary Graham. Lady Mary had a house in Hanover Square and, as the wife of Frances's mother's only brother, she had graciously offered to introduce her niece into society. Lady Mary was English, the daughter of an earl, and very well established in high society. Her marble hall was filled as Douglas, dressed in evening attire, came in the great front door. There was a rainbow of color, the sound of expensive fabrics rustling, the scent of many different perfumes, and the noise of chatter. Frances stood with her aunt and uncle on the wide landing at the top of the stairs, greeting her guests as their turns came to be presented.

Douglas never remembered what she was wearing, only that it was white and fell gracefully about her tall, slim figure. Her ash-gold hair was caught in combs off her face with just a few tendrils allowed to escape and curl on her cheek. Douglas felt an ache at the back of his throat as he looked at her.

"Douglas!" There was a flash of very white teeth as she smiled at him. "It's so nice to see someone I know," she said sincerely.

"I don't think you will lack company, Frances," he answered dryly.

She held his hand for a minute longer, then the major-domo boomed "His Grace the Duke of Grafton and Her Grace the Duchess." Frances turned to greet them and Douglas passed on to the Reception Room. The crystal chandeliers were ablaze with light and the French windows which led in to the garden at the back of the house were opened, as it was a warm night. Viscount Winburton, who had preceded Douglas through the line, turned to him, "Did I hear Miss Stewart say she knew you?"

"That's right," Douglas replied calmly. "Since she was twelve years old, in fact. I'm Douglas Macdonald and I live with the Macdonalds of Lochaber. Lady Lochaber is Miss Stewart's godmother."

"I'm Winburton." The young man held out his hand.

"Where did she come from?" he asked dazedly. "I've never seen a more beautiful girl."

It was a refrain Douglas was to hear all that night and throughout the following weeks. At every ball Frances went to she was surrounded by a throng of men. Her admirers included all of the most eligible bachelors in London: a duke, a duke's heir, a marquis, two viscounts, an earl, and an earl's heir, to name the most prominent. Frances's religion was obviously more than made up for by her beauty, her charm, and her modestly respectable inheritance. In fact the atmosphere among those vying for her attention rapidly became extremely tense, with each one jealously looking for a special sign that would show where her favor really lay. Young as she was, however, Frances was quite experienced in fending off overly enthusiastic admirers. She was friendly to everyone and sentimental with no one.

Douglas watched her play this dangerous game with growing alarm. She had a purpose in this elaborate London debut. He could see it in the dense green of her eyes and in the defiant tilt of her perfect jaw. The marriage proposals poured in and all Frances would ever say was "I'm not sure I wish to marry anyone. I need to see a little more of the world before I make such a difficult decision. Please don't speak of it yet." And she would smile her enchanting smile and leave them waiting. And hoping.

Douglas was almost certain that this effortless collection of would-be husbands was for Ian's benefit. He was a younger son, poor enough to need a profession to increase his income, and only twenty years of age. The contrast between his status and her London admirers would be enough to give anyone pause. She seemed to be at pains to demonstrate that if he didn't want to marry her, there were plenty of others who did. It was the only reason Douglas could find to account for her behavior; Frances did not ordinarily try to exploit her beauty. He was certain she had no real interest in any of the men who dogged her footsteps. Until Robert Sedburgh entered the picture.

It was Charlie who introduced them. Lord Robert was in Alan's regiment and had sought Charlie out to offer his regrets over Alan's death. Lord Robert was himself on leave in order to recuperate from a shoulder wound. He had been staying with his parents, the Earl and Countess of Aysgarth, and had come up to London now that he was recovered. He looked up Charlie and Charlie brought him along to the Eversly Ball. It was there he met Frances for the first time.

Robert Sedburgh was one of the most likable men of his time. His thoughtfulness in seeking out Charlie to speak of Alan was typical of his character. He was tall, fair-haired and blue-eyed, with a warmly attractive smile. He would one day inherit immense wealth and large estates. He served as an aide to Lord Wellington and was due to return to the Peninsula as soon as he had completely regained his health. Then he met Frances.

He had more success than the rest of her followers. Frances really liked him. It would be hard not to. He was witty, charming, handsome, and twenty-six years of age. He was a man who would occupy a position of great responsibility, great opportunity, great wealth, and great power. His wife would be a woman of great consideration. A girl might do much worse than trust herself to such a man. It seemed to Douglas that Frances was tempted.

"When shall I wish you happy?" he said to her one day in the sunny back room of her aunt's house where he was painting her portrait.

She was normally a good subject, sitting quietly upright in the pose he had suggested, but now she turned her head. "What do you mean?"

"I mean when are you going to accept Robert Sedburgh?"

Her eyebrows raised a trifle. "He hasn't asked me," she said. Then, as he continued to look at her, the corners of her mouth deepened. "He hasn't had the chance," she admitted.

"He will find one."

"I suppose so."

He put his brush down. "Frances," he said gently, "if you don't want Lord Robert, what do you want?"

Her hands moved restlessly and then were still again. She raised her chin and looked at him. Her eyes were somber. "You know me too well, Douglas."

"My question still stands."

She got up and walked to the window. With her back to him she said "I want Ian of course. But I want him here, with me, not off in some other country fighting somebody else's war."

"You said yourself he won't go to the Peninsula."

She turned around to face him. "Not while his mother keeps him to his promise. But how long, Douglas, do you think she'll hold out against him? You know what Ian is like when he wants something. Determined. Ruthless even. He succeeded in getting himself thrown out of Cambridge. Now that he's out of school he'll raise more hell than Scotland's seen since the '45. She'll give in. Ian's her favorite. She could never stand up against him.''

He looked at her suddenly bleak face. ''The very qualities you love Ian for are the ones you're trying to smash, Frances,'' he said gently. ''If you want a kind, gentle, calm, considerate man who will unfailingly put your wishes and your welfare before his own, marry Robert Sedburgh. He will cherish and guard you all his life. You'll be safe with him.''

Her face was closed and aloof. ''I don't care about being safe.''

''Yes, you do,'' he contradicted her. ''You want to keep Ian safe, at any rate. But you would smother him, Frances. Ian doesn't want to feel safe. He wants to feel alive.''

''He doesn't need to go to war to feel alive,'' she said bitterly.

''No, but he needs to feel he is using his brains, his courage, his determination. He needs to feel *extended*, Frances.'' He leaned forward, doing his best for Ian, trying to make her understand. ''He loves you, you know that. But it isn't enough, Frances. It would be for Robert Sedburgh. But not for Ian.''

He looked at her pale set face. She knew that, he thought. It was what she could not forgive.

Chapter Four

We twa hae run about the braes
    And pou'd the gowans fine,
But we've wander'd monie a weary fit
    Sin' auld lang syne.

—ROBERT BURNS

The Countess of Pemberly gave a ball in early July that was one of the highlights of that year's season. By this time betting in the clubs was heavily in favor of Robert Sedburgh's being accepted by the reigning belle, Frances Stewart. Lord Robert himself was only waiting for the appropriate opportunity to speak to Frances. He had already declared himself to her uncle.

"I wish you luck, Sedburgh," Alexander Graham had said with amusement. "If I had a pound for every man in this town who wants to marry Frances, I'd be a rich man."

"I know," Lord Robert had replied ruefully. "I can only say she won't find a man who loves her more than I do."

Alexander had clapped him on the shoulder. "If she

25

has any sense she'll take you, boy. But I'm afraid Frances is like her mother. You can't count on her doing the sensible thing when it comes to marriage. And her father will let her do as she pleases. Within reason, of course.''

Lord Robert had some reason to believe that he pleased Frances, and it was with a mixture of hope and apprehension that he asked her to walk out into the garden with him about halfway through the Pemberly ball.

Frances was feeling restless and unsettled and was not as careful as she usually was. Her refusal to give Lord Robert an opening was not part of a calculated game; it came, rather, from a certain fear. He was not a man one could take lightly. But tonight she was feeling oppressed by the crush of people and the heat, and she agreed to step outside with him.

They walked to the small fountain that stood in the center of the garden, and Frances took a deep breath. ''It is lovely out here,'' she said, delicately touching a rose that bloomed on a bush close beside her.

''It's enchanting,'' he replied sincerely, looking at her.

''You're easily enchanted, my lord,'' Frances said smiling.

''No, I'm not easily enchanted.'' He paused a minute. ''But you've enchanted me, Miss Stewart.'' He reached out and took her hand. ''My feelings can't be unknown to you,'' he continued quietly. ''It would give me enormous happiness if you would consent to be my wife.''

Imperceptibly she had stiffened. ''I would never marry a soldier,'' said Frances.

He smiled in relief. ''Is that all? But of course I

wouldn't expect you to marry a man who was going off to war. I should resign my commission. We would live at Aysgarth; my mother and father would love you. But if you decided you didn't want to live with them, we could live wherever you chose. I have a great number of houses. Or I could buy another one. It shall all be just as you wish."

Frances looked at him with inscrutable eyes. "You would give up the army for me?"

"I would do anything for you, Miss Stewart," said Robert Sedburgh in the kindest, tenderest voice Frances had ever heard. "I love you."

She dropped her eyes. "I thank you more than I can say for your offer," she replied at last. "It does me great honor."

"Don't say that," he begged. "Just say yes." The moonlight turned his fair hair to silver. His eyes as he looked at her were very blue. "You do like me, rather, don't you?" he said.

"I like you very much, Lord Robert. But marriage . . ." She looked up at him, eyes dark in her moon-bleached face. "I don't know. It is a very difficult question."

"You don't have to answer it right away. Think it over for as long as may be necessary. If I can profit by waiting I'll gladly wait. Only remember that in the end my dearest happiness depends on your answer."

Frances bowed her head. "I will remember, my lord. Only, don't think me unkind if I ask you to say no more about this for awhile."

"I wouldn't distress you for the world," he said. "Shall we go in now? The next set is starting, I believe."

She smiled at him gratefully and walked with him

back through the tall French doors and into the ballroom. There were a number of speculative glances turned on the two fair heads as they came in, but neither Frances's nor Lord Robert's expression gave anything away. She was claimed by her next partner and Lord Robert went to get himself a glass of champagne.

It was half an hour later, the music had just stopped, and Frances was still standing on the floor with the Marquis of Bermington when there was a little stir by the door of the ballroom. Lady Pemberly, Frances's hostess, was standing beside her. "Goodness, who is that?" the countess said. "I'm quite sure he wasn't on my invitation list." Frances turned to look.

The boy in the doorway was very tall, and dark as a gypsy with untamed eyes and a sensual, proud mouth. His dark eyes were searching the room methodically and when they reached Frances Stewart they stopped. Lady Pemberly, watching, saw the almost physical impact made by those locking gazes. Then the tall youngster came directly across the floor, with long, arrogant steps, his head up, his brows drawn together in an angry line. He appeared to be totally unconscious of any watching eyes. When he reached Frances he put a none-too-gentle hand on her arm. "I have to talk to you," he said without preamble. "Come along. There's a room off the upper landing."

"Miss Stewart." It was Lord Bermington. "Shall I send this fellow on his way?"

"No. Ian!" As he pressed forward Frances put a restraining hand on his forearm, feeling the hard muscle underneath the correct black evening coat. "It's all right, Lord Bermington," she said. "I know him. It's Ian Macdonald, Lochaber's brother."

28

Ian's eyes went from the marquis's face back to Frances. His hand tightened on her arm. The watching circle was aware of the intense feeling, part hostile, part something else, that vibrated between the girl and boy. "I'm coming," she said, and went back across the polished floor with him, her slender body straight as a lance.

Neither of them spoke until Ian had closed the door of the small anteroom behind them. Then Frances said, "You do choose your moments, don't you?"

The face she looked at was set and stern and the dark eyes held a glitter in their depths that caused her breath to quicken. "I got a letter from Douglas," he said. "I came immediately. What the bloody hell are you up to, Frances?"

Her eyes widened innocently. "I don't know what you are talking about. I am making a come-out. Plenty of other girls do that."

"You are not plenty of other girls," he said grimly. "You're my girl. Douglas told me you've been collecting suitors faster than Penelope. What are you trying to do? Teach me a lesson?"

"I wouldn't dream of doing that, Ian," she said sweetly. "Anyone clever enough to get himself sent down from Cambridge doesn't need lessons from me."

His eyes narrowed in comprehension. "Ah. I had a feeling that was what the problem was."

"Problem?" She was annoyed to hear her voice was shaking. "What problem? The fact that you are making a mess of your life? The fact that you have thrown away your best chance for the future? The fact that you obviously don't care about my feelings? I don't see any problem."

29

He looked at her once more and then turned and prowled up and down the room. "I couldn't take it any more," he said finally, coming to stand before her. "I was so bloody bored."

"And just what is it you won't find equally boring, Ian?" she asked steadily.

His smile transformed his face. "You," he said. "What are you doing in London, Frances? If you want to marry someone, marry me. There's no point in our waiting another year now that I'm not going back to school." He put his hands on her shoulders. "I must admit I had that thought in mind when I—er—parted from Cambridge."

For a long moment she stood still, feeling the warmth of his fingers on her bare flesh, the sudden tumult of her heart. Ian could always do this to her. "Have you given up trying to get your mother to buy you a commission?" she said breathlessly.

His face hardened. "No." He slid his hands down her arms. "But you could come out to Lisbon with me. A number of officers' wives are living there. I'd get back on leave to see you."

"Or maybe you'd come back like Alan. Permanently. In a coffin."

"Frances . . ." he said low. "I love you."

"No, Ian," she said, and tried to draw away from him.

"Come here."

"No," she said again, but by now he had an arm around her, pinning her arms down and pressing her head back against his shoulder. She stiffened against him, but he only held her more tightly, forcing her lips up to his. His kiss was hard and demanding. She could feel the strength of his body pressed against hers. Slowly she relaxed against him, surrendering to the wild singing in her own blood. She kissed him back. They were so totally absorbed in each other that neither one of them heard the door open.

"For God's sake, Ian," said Douglas. "You could have a thought for Frances's reputation even if you have none for your own."

The two of them looked at him as if they didn't recognize him. Then Frances laughed. "When did you ever know Ian to care about the opinion of others, Douglas?" There was a recklessness in her laugh that made Douglas look at her more closely. She was still standing close to Ian, so close, he saw, that her shoulder was touching his arm. Her eyes glowed and there was warm color in her cheeks and lips; she looked utterly beautiful.

Ian grinned, a boy's grin. "I thought you wanted me to come. You were the one who wrote to tell me what was going on here."

"I didn't mean you to arrive in the middle of the season's biggest crush and drag Frances off the floor into a private room," Douglas responded crossly. "How did you know this room was here anyway?"

"I asked the major-domo," Ian replied simply, and Frances laughed again.

"Well, you're both going back to the ballroom now. Together. It will be worse if it looks as if I had to bring you back. Then, Ian, you will turn Frances over to me. Fortunately it is my dance. Now go. I'll join you in two minutes."

His air of urgency made an impression on the girl and boy. They exchanged a glance and then Ian shrugged.

"Oh, all right. Come on, Frances. I'll come around to see you tomorrow." They left the anteroom together, and when Douglas reached the ballroom he saw the two of them talking to Robert Sedburgh.

"Oh, there you are, Frances," said Douglas as he came up to them. "My dance, I believe." He turned to Ian and held out his hand. "How are you, Ian? It's just like you to crash a party. When did you get to London and where are you staying?"

Ian's dark eyes were aflame with laughter. "To answer your questions, Douglas, I am fine, I arrived in London about an hour ago, and I am staying with you."

"Oh, you are?"

"Yes. Your man told me where I could find you, so I put on my evening gear and came. Who is the Countess of Pemberly anyway?"

"Oh dear," said Frances, her social conscience finally stung. "You must find her and introduce yourself, Ian. Crashing a party is one thing, but totally ignoring one's hostess is unforgivable."

"I'll introduce him to Lady Pemberly, Miss Stewart," offered Lord Robert.

Frances smiled at him. "That is very kind of you, my lord."

Ian's eyes were on the assembled company. "Good God," he said in a startled tone, "who is the old duck in the purple turban?"

Frances giggled and Douglas took her firmly by the elbow and led her onto the floor. "What are you up to?" he asked her severely.

She treated him to a wide, innocent gaze. "Everybody seems to be asking me that question tonight."

"You look like a cat that swallowed the cream," he

told her. "Did Ian promise you to stay out of the army?"

"No." A shadow crossed her face and then was gone. "But he will," she said positively.

Douglas was not so sure.

Chapter Five

O stay at hame, my noble lord!
O stay at hame, my marrow!

—ANONYMOUS

Frances awoke the next morning with a bubble of happiness inside herself. *He came, he came,* she hummed over and over beneath her breath. *He wants to marry me.* The problem of Ian's still-evident desire to join the army she brushed aside. She had felt her power over Robert Sedburgh last night. If he was willing to give up the army for her sake, why should not Ian? She decided to write a letter to her father. Surely he could get Ian into the University of Edinburgh.

At about the same time that Frances was happily laying her plans Ian was saying to Douglas "How can I get Frances off by herself for a while, Douglas?"

"You can't," his cousin replied bluntly. "This is not Castle Hunter, Ian, and Lady Mary Graham is not your mother. She keeps a close eye on Frances. You may perhaps be permitted to drive her in the park, but only at the hour when half of London is there as well."

Ian frowned. "You don't mean it."

"I do."

Ian took a hearty helping of sausage. "Well, when Lady Mary discovers I am going to marry Frances she'll loosen up."

"Has Frances said she'll marry you?" Douglas asked carefully.

Ian swallowed his sausage and raised his coffee cup. "Not yet. But she will. She's got this fixation about me not joining the army. I'll have to persuade her."

"You'll have to persuade your mother first," Douglas said dryly.

Ian grinned, his teeth very white in his dark face. "If Frances says she'll marry me, mother will come round."

"Is that why you want to marry her?" Douglas said harshly. "To force your mother into buying you a commission?"

Ian put down his cup and looked at Douglas. "What a stupid thing to say." His voice was quiet and very hard.

Douglas's eyes fell before that swordlike look. "It was, rather. I'm sorry."

Ian began to eat again. "What else is there to do in this town besides courting Frances?"

Douglas sighed. "The same things there are in Edinburgh, only more of them."

Ian looked bleak. "God, Douglas, if I don't find something to do with myself soon I shall go mad! Or die at an early age from too much drink."

His cousin laughed. "How are things in Scotland?"

"Not good," Ian said grimly. "More and more landlords are bringing in sheep. All they want is to take as much of the profits as they can and spend it all in

36

London. No one is plowing anything back into the land. I'm sorry to say that my brother is as bad as the rest of them. Consequently there are more and more people living on smaller and smaller pieces of land. And no one is trying to do anything to remedy the situation.''

"I know," Douglas said quietly.

"That's one of the reasons I want to get away, Douglas," Ian said desperately. "I can't bear to see what is happening to the Highlands. And it is our own leaders who are doing it. The disaster of the '45 will be as nothing compared to what is coming now. And there's not a damn thing I can do about it.''

"I know," Douglas said again.

Frances was sitting in her aunt's drawing room with Lady Mary, the Marquis of Bermington, and the Earl of Chilton when Ian arrived in Hanover Square that afternoon. He paused on the threshold, a startled look on his face as he took in the room's inhabitants. "Ian!" Frances looked lit from within as she said his name.

"I didn't realize you were holding court, Frances," he said, moving across the room with a catlike grace unusual in so big a man.

She gave his hand a warning squeeze. "I don't think you know my aunt, Lady Mary Graham. Aunt Mary, may I present Mr. Ian Macdonald.''

"How do you do, Mr. Macdonald," Lady Mary said discouragingly. She was a small, dark woman and her eyes widened slightly as he came across to bow over her hand. "Goodness, but you're big!''

Ian smiled charmingly. It was part of his policy to make a good impression on Lady Mary. "I am so pleased to meet you, Lady Mary," he said in his deep, slow voice.

Frances introduced him to Lord Bermington and Lord Chilton and invited him to sit down. He was eight years younger than Chilton and twelve years younger than Bermington, but both those sophisticated men of the world paled beside his intensely alive presence. He sat down, crossed his arms, and lifted an ironic eyebrow at Frances. Your move, his eyes said to her unmistakably.

"I promised Ian I would drive out with him today, Aunt Mary," she said promptly.

"But Miss Stewart, I thought you were driving with me," protested Lord Chilton.

"I am so sorry, my lord," said Frances with sweet earnestness. "But Mr. Macdonald and I are childhood friends, you understand. We haven't seen each other in ages and we have so much catching up to do. How is your mother, Ian?" she asked, turning to him.

"Very well, Frances," he answered gravely, but his eyes glinted with amusement.

"I'm so glad. You must tell me all about Castle Hunter." She rose. "If you'll excuse me, Aunt Mary, gentlemen, I will go and get my hat."

She exited gracefully, leaving Ian to face the hostile glances of two English nobles. "How do you know Miss Stewart?" Lord Bermington asked suspiciously.

Ian stared at him with unruffled composure. He had always been a good winner. "My mother is Miss Stewart's godmother," he said agreeably. "We have known each other since we were children."

"That can't have been very long ago," snapped Lord Chilton, looking at the young face before him.

Ian looked at him appraisingly and Chilton found

himself growing red. He was of medium height and slightly chubby, and Ian's gaze spoke volumes. Fortunately Frances reappeared and the three men rose, Ian towering over the other two.

Frances gave a shrewd look around and said, "I'm ready." She and Ian went down the stairs and out the front door.

"You're lucky I happen to have a phaeton with me," he informed her as they went. "What would you have done if I'd walked?"

"Walked with you, I expect," she answered serenely.

And so, feeling very pleased with themselves and with each other, they went out driving together.

They quarrelled the whole time.

Ian and Frances were the subject of several conversations that evening. Robert Sedburgh was dining at White's with Viscount Morton and Henry Farringdon when the topic came up. All three men had, at one time or another, proposed marriage to Frances, and normally they found the best way to preserve their friendship was to avoid talking about her. However, a new contestant had entered the race for her hand and they all found themselves intensely curious. "I saw Macdonald driving Miss Stewart in the park this afternoon," offered Lord Morton.

"Did you?" Mr. Farringdon raised an inquisitive eyebrow. "You were the only one of us to meet him, Rob. He's a childhood friend of hers, or so I heard. What did you think?"

"He put on quite a performance last night for a childhood friend," Lord Morton put in before Lord

Robert could answer. "He continued it this afternoon, I might add."

Both of his listeners put down their forks and stared at him. "What happened?" asked Lord Robert.

"Well, they weren't getting along, that's for sure. Macdonald looked like a thundercloud."

"What about Miss Stewart?"

"Oh, she was making an effort to hide her feelings. She noticed about half the people who greeted her." There was a pause. "She looked furious."

"Well, that's good news," Mr. Farringdon said hopefully.

"Is it?" Lord Robert looked at Lord Morton. "Did it seem like a childhood friends, brother-and-sister kind of quarrel to you, John?"

"No." Lord Morton looked sober. "No. It didn't look like that at all. I don't quite know what the relationship between those two is, but it definitely isn't that of brother and sister."

"Hell!" said Mr. Farringdon violently.

"Yes," responded Lord Robert. "Quite."

"Hell!" said Ian as he slammed his riding crop down on a table. "What's the matter with Frances, Douglas? She never used to be like this."

Douglas looked up from the book he was reading. "You didn't persuade her, I gather," he said mildly.

"It's like talking to a wall!" Ian stormed. "She's as bad as my mother—no—worse. 'If you really loved me, Ian, you would promise me to stay out of the army.' Christ! It doesn't seem to occur to her that if she loved me she wouldn't try to blackmail me."

Douglas looked at the dark, stormy face before him. "She's afraid for you, Ian."

Ian sat down in a chair and moodily contemplated his long, booted legs. "I know." He looked up at Douglas, a sardonic glint in his eyes. "She wants me to go to the University of Edinburgh and study law. She says her father can get me in. I ask you, Douglas, do you see me as a lawyer?"

Douglas smiled. "No. I don't."

"The University of Edinburgh," Ian said in derision. "I should die of the tedium. The only reason I lasted at Cambridge for as long as I did was because . . ." he looked quickly at Douglas and then shrugged. "Oh, it doesn't matter."

Douglas sat up in his chair. "Go on," he said. "You've whetted my curiosity."

"I didn't mean to." Then, as Douglas continued to look at him expectantly, he relented. "Oh, it was the wife of one of the bigwigs. I had begun to wonder if there was something wrong with me. From what I heard I was the only eighteen-year-old boy at school who had never had a woman." He frowned. "It was Frances, I suppose. I was too involved with her to think of anyone else."

"I know," said Douglas without expression.

Ian flashed him a sharp look but continued. "Anyway, I was beginning to think I had a problem. Then I met—ah, well, I met *her*. It was an experience." Ian grinned reminiscently. "I learned more from her than I ever did in the lecture room. She told me I may have to face a lot of problems in my life, but *that* most definitely wouldn't be one of them. She was very reassuring."

Douglas stared at him for a few minutes without

speaking. Ian was contemplating his boots once more and Douglas had a good view of the hard line of his young cheek, shadowed by his down-looking black lashes. There was a sense of power unleashed about Ian. It was what gave his presence its remarkable intensity. And he's only twenty years old, thought Douglas inconsequently. Ian suddenly rose to his feet. "Anyway, she doesn't really matter," he said. "Only Frances matters. And I don't know what to do about her."

"She isn't going to change, Ian," Douglas said reluctantly. "You're two of a kind, I'm afraid. She said you were ruthless when you went after what you wanted. She is too. You've just never come up against her before."

Surprise flickered in Ian's eyes. "Have you?"

A rueful smile crept into Douglas's eyes. "Oh yes. Frances doesn't change, Ian. Under her charm and her serenity she is adamant. She hasn't changed about you, although she's had all of Edinburgh and now all of London camping on her doorstep. She won't change, either. You should have heard her attack Lord Bermington for a remark he made about you last night."

Ian's eyes had a faintly ironical contraction. "Oh, she's never allowed anyone to point a finger of criticism at me. She thinks, I imagine, that she can see to that well enough herself."

Douglas felt a savage pain around his heart. "Don't you think she's worth making a few sacrifices for, Ian?" he asked suddenly.

Ian stared back at him, a look of alarming grimness about his mouth. "If Frances wants a safe, peaceful life with someone who will agree with every word she says, she'd better marry that Sedburgh fellow she was throw-

42

ing in my face this afternoon. Not me." He strode out of the room, and Douglas leaned back in his chair and closed his eyes. He had, he remembered, given Frances the same advice himself.

Chapter Six

Robin was a rovin boy

—ROBERT BURNS

Douglas did not see Ian for the rest of the evening. He discovered in the morning that Charlie had taken him to a new gambling hell that had acquired a rather unsavory reputation.

"Did you lose much money?" Douglas asked over the breakfast table.

"No. Charlie did, though. He's a fool," said Lord Lochaber's younger brother. "I will say the wine was good. I drank too much of it." Ian helped himself to some salmon.

"You look remarkably fit for one who was out carousing till all hours."

Ian looked amused. "Douglas. I was with Charlie. Charlie's idea of a wild carouse is my idea of a quiet evening. I drank too much out of boredom."

Douglas put down his cup. "Is that why you're staying with me? Because I'm more of a devil than Charlie is?"

Ian laughed. "You aren't what I'd call a hell-raiser,

Douglas, but your conversation is infinitely preferable to Charlie's. Ten minutes of him and I'm halfway into a coma.''

''Your devotion to me is truly moving,'' his cousin said with mock solemnity.

''Stow it, Douglas,'' Ian returned inelegantly.

There was a companionable silence as both men systematically ate their way through breakfast. All the Macdonalds had healthy appetites. Then Douglas said, ''What are you doing today?''

''Charlie has his uses,'' Ian returned. ''He's taking me to Jackson's boxing saloon. What about you?''

''I am painting Frances this morning,'' said Douglas imperturbably.

Ian's black brows contracted. ''Are you? Well, I hope she's in a better temper than she was yesterday.''

''She will be. The only person Frances is ever out of temper with is you.''

''I know,'' Ian said gloomily. ''I know.''

Ian had a very satisfactory morning. He met three of Frances's suitors at Jackson's and they made the mistake of challenging him. Lord Morton was the first. He assumed, like all the others, that Ian's youth and probable inexperience would more than compensate for his obvious physical strength. He had a moment's doubt when he saw the breadth of those shoulders and that strongly muscled chest, but decided almost immediately that his own superior science would triumph.

He was wrong. So were the Earl of March and Lord Barrow. Ian did not rush enthusiastically to his own defeat, as everyone had securely expected. He played his opponents along, waiting with watchful competence for his opening. When it came he took it without hesitation.

He felt in a much better humor afterwards and spent a pleasant hour sparring with the great Jackson himself. That worthy had been anxious to discover who Ian's teacher had been.

"I learned from a book," said Ian laconically and with perfect truth. "Then I practiced with the crofter's lads back home. Now, they are tough." He looked scornfully at the flower of English manhood assembled around him that morning.

"I'd like to meet some of those lads," said Jackson.

"They'd like fine to meet you," returned Ian, with his endearing boyish grin.

Frances dressed with particular care for the ball she was going to that evening. Douglas had promised to bring Ian. She chose a dress of pale green feather-light gauze, cut, as she thought, daringly low. She sat patiently while her aunt's dresser coaxed her magnificent ash-gold hair into a knot high on her head from which a few curls were allowed to fall artistically. When the maid had finished Frances looked appraisingly in the tall glass. "I'll do," she said.

The dresser looked at the girl before her. "Yes, miss," she said dryly. "You'll do."

Frances was, as usual, besieged for dances as soon as she and Lady Mary made their appearance in the ballroom. She smiled and responded and all the while kept an eye out for Ian. He arrived with Douglas shortly after eleven. He came in, looking tall even in that room full of people, saw her dancing with Robert Sedburgh, and settled back to wait for the end of the set.

Lord Robert saw him too. "I see your friend Mr. Macdonald has come in," he observed to Frances. "I understand he was wreaking havoc at Jackson's boxing saloon this afternoon."

She frowned. "What do you mean?"

"Merely that Mr. Macdonald is extremely talented. Jackson was very impressed."

Frances suddenly chuckled; she had a marvelous laugh, soft and warm and infectious. "He probably wanted to hit me," she said candidly. "If I know Ian, though, he's feeling much better. Knocking a few bodies about has always done wonders for his disposition."

Lord Robert looked a little shocked. Unconsciously he had expected Frances to disapprove of Ian's fighting. All the women he knew did. Or at least they pretended to. Frances looked at his face and suddenly sobered. "I don't think I should suit you, Lord Robert. I really don't think I should."

"Don't say that," he responded with unaccustomed harshness.

The set had come to an end, and Ian was coming toward them. Lord Robert looked from her to the approaching boy with inscrutable blue eyes. His smile was not welcoming.

Ian didn't notice. "Have you saved me some dances, Frances?" he asked her, his black brows quizzical.

"Yes, the ones you requested," she lied. Her voice was mild but the green eyes were imperious. "You're just in time to claim this next quadrille."

Ian looked into the familiar glinting green and gave her a look he meant to be casually amused. Lord Robert, however, caught a glimpse of Ian's glance, and the expression in those dark eyes made him catch his breath.

He did not need to wonder any longer about the nature of Ian Macdonald's feelings for Frances. And he was sensitive enough to appreciate that in this tall, black-haired boy he had a formidable rival.

After Ian finished dancing with Frances he looked around for Douglas. His cousin was conversing seriously with a broad, ruddy-faced man, and when he saw Ian he beckoned. Douglas's companion was Col. Richard Frost, one of the mainstays of the Horse Guards, and Ian eagerly joined in what he found to be an absorbing discussion of the Peninsula War.

They talked through three sets. Frances, dancing again with Lord Robert, looked for the twentieth time at the trio in the window and asked, "Who is that man Douglas and Ian Macdonald are talking to?"

Lord Robert looked. "Colonel Frost. He's at the Horse Guards."

Frances gazed steadily at the three men, her fine brows drawn together, her face intent and stern. "Oh. The Horse Guards."

"Is anything wrong, Miss Stewart?" Lord Robert asked with concern.

"No." She gave him a brief, strained smile and changed the topic.

Ian's conversation was interrupted by his hostess, who arrived and ruthlessly bore him off to be introduced to one of the forgotten debutantes whom Frances's success had relegated to the sidelines.

Miss Abbott was seventeen, reasonably pretty and very shy. She acknowledged Lady Hester's introduction with a blush and looked, worshipfully but not very hopefully, at Ian. She had danced only twice that evening.

If she had been a beauty Ian would have unhesitat-

49

ingly extricated himself, but those shy brown eyes appealed to his essentially kind heart. He got Miss Abbott a glass of punch and then asked her to dance.

"You are a friend of Miss Stewart's, are you not?" she asked diffidently as they danced.

"Yes." Ian looked at the wistful small face turned up to him. The top of Miss Abbott's head just reached his shoulder. "Miss Stewart should be ashamed of monopolizing all the eligible men the way she does," he said sympathetically. "It must make life difficult for all the rest of you pretty girls."

Miss Abbott blushed even harder at being called a pretty girl. "She can't help it, I expect. She is so beautiful. She always reminds me of some lines of poetry I once heard. 'Was this the face that launched a thousand ships and burnt the topless towers of Illium?' " At Ian's amused glance she blushed even more furiously.

"Do you know Miss Stewart?" he asked, tactfully ignoring her confusion.

"No. We have never been introduced."

"I'll introduce you," he said decisively. Frances would know how to manage things for small Miss Abbott. He smiled at her reassuringly. "You'll like her. She is much nicer than Helen of Troy."

So he ushered his innocent little chick over to meet Frances, who was expectedly efficient. Without quite knowing how it had happened, Miss Abbott found herself dancing with the Earl of Chilton, engaged to dance with three other men, and spoken for for supper by Lord Robert Sedburgh, who had already ascertained that Frances was engaged.

Ian took Frances into supper, and as they walked together toward the room Lady Hester had set aside for refreshments he looked with approval at her figure, slim and supple in its pale green gown. "Thank God you're tall," he remarked. "I have a crick in my neck from talking to Miss Abbott."

She shot him a look from under her remarkable lashes. She was burning to know what he had been saying to Colonel Frost, but decided to hold her peace. She didn't want another public quarrel with Ian, and that topic would invariably lead to argument.

"I have to thank you for sharing your worshippers with her," he continued. "The poor little thing looked quite forlorn."

She looked up into his face, a smile on her lips but a certain gravity in her eyes. "*You* don't worship me, do you Ian?"

He returned her look, unsmiling, and for a minute they were alone in the middle of Lady Hester's crowded ballroom. "No. I don't worship you," he said. His deep voice was calm. "I love you."

Two girls left the ball that evening with their thoughts on Ian. In the coach that was taking them home Mrs. Abbott ran on enthusiastically about all her daughter's noble partners and their prospects. Miss Abbott listened quietly, but her mind was filled with the memory of a dark face with hard, exciting cheekbones and a sensual arrogant mouth. In her opinion, no one she had ever met was half so magnificent as Ian Macdonald.

Frances worried all night about Ian's conversation with Colonel Frost. Toward the end of the ball, however, Ian had had a momentous meeting with someone else that was to have a far more lasting effect on both their lives. He had met the young man who was representing in London the newly declared independent country of Venezuela. The man's name was Simón Bolívar.

Chapter Seven

Had we never lov'd sae kindly
Had we never lov'd sae blindly,
Never met—or never parted,
We had n'er been broken-hearted.

—ROBERT BURNS

Bolívar, the future liberator of Spanish America, was at this time twenty-eight years of age and poised upon the initial undertaking of his great enterprise. He had come to London to try to win British aid for Venezuela, but Britain was allied to Spain at the time and Spain was not pleased with the developing situation in South America. Venezuela had voted for independence on April 19; Buenos Aires had followed on May 25; and Santa Fe de Bogotá and Santiago de Chile would declare themselves within two months. The Spanish-speaking New World was following the inspiration of the United States of America and Bolívar envisioned a great new country to be called Colombia and to be modeled after the successful American example. He was a man with a dream, and in Ian he found an eager listener. The two young men spent many hours together.

Frances knew nothing of South America and saw nothing to object to in Ian's pleasure in Colonel Bolívar's company. Douglas, who was much more politically aware than she, was concerned but held his tongue.

Several weeks went by, and the impasse between Ian and Frances still stood. Ian found himself drawn into a daily round that consisted of club in the morning, calls or a ride in the afternoon, dinner parties and balls in the evening followed by whatever else he could find to occupy himself until three or four in the morning when he would tumble, not tired enough, into bed. As the days went by he felt within himself a growing longing to get away, away from the gossip and the talk of war and the talk of government policy, away from the suffocation of conforming to armchair social rules. If he should lose Frances—he did not see how he could bear to live without Frances. But neither could he bear to live with her, not under the terms she would impose. He needed to get away from it all, to breathe again. He longed wildly to be gone from London.

A break in the stalemate occurred when both Ian and Frances received an invitation to join a house party at Wick, home of the Earl and Countess of Darlington. Lady Darlington had brought out her daughter Catherine that year and, along with the other mothers of marriageable daughters, she couldn't wait to see Frances safely out of competition. She had her eye on Lord Robert Sedburgh for Catherine and was not at all pleased by his obvious predilection for Frances. However, she had not missed Frances's equally obvious predilection for Ian. Lady Darlington therefore evolved a very simple policy:

throw Frances and Ian together as often as possible, preferably under the jealous eye of Lord Robert. This strategy resulted in a series of invitations that surprised all the recipients. However, they accepted.

Wick was in Surrey, so it was not much of a journey. Lady Mary Graham accompanied Frances. She was in favor of Robert Sedburgh's suit and was pleased when Lady Darlington had said he would be present. She was not pleased when Ian arrived. She had not expected him. She couldn't help but like Ian; women always did. But she did not want her niece to marry him, a younger son with no prospects. Frances could do so much better.

The first few days of the house party were tense. Frances spent a good deal of time with Lord Robert and avoided Ian. The result of this tactic was to put him into a savage temper, which he alleviated by riding hard all day and drinking more than was good for him at night. After three days of this he determined to have it out with Frances.

Lady Darlington had arranged an afternoon riding expedition which consisted of herself, Lord Thorndon, Catherine, Lord Robert, Frances, and Ian. They were to go as far as Rudgwick, but after they were out for an hour the sky clouded over and darkened ominously. Lady Darlington insisted they turn around and head for home. She also managed to arrange things so that Catherine and Lord Robert rode together, with herself and Lord Thorndon following. This left Frances and Ian to bring up the rear.

Frances was fully aware of Ian's growing fury, which she regarded with considerable satisfaction. She would teach him that others were willing to accede to her wishes even if he continued to be stubborn. Since she had a healthy respect for the temper she was so blatantly provoking she took care to keep from being left alone with him. She had felt Lady Darlington's presence as chaperone would be protection enough on the horseback expedition. She had not reckoned with the countess's ambition for her daughter, which thrust Frances into Ian's company, nor had she reckoned fully with his ruthless ability to go after what he wanted. To her dismay she found herself alone in the middle of a wood with Ian; the others were about a quarter of a mile ahead of them and it would have been undignified to shout for help when he laid his hand on her bridle and brought her horse to a halt.

For five minutes she sat in speechless indignation while he told her in no uncertain terms what he thought of her manners, her morals, her intelligence, and her plans for the future. Then, her eyes flashing green fire, she shouted, "You don't own me, Ian Macdonald!" and, wrenching her horse's head around, hit him with her crop and galloped down the path toward the river.

He stared after her for a minute, his face black with anger, and then he swore furiously. He had been this way yesterday. *The bloody bridge is out,* he thought and he drove urgent heels into his own horse's flanks. There had been flooding in the area due to heavy rains, and Ian had noticed the small sign posted on the bridge yesterday. Frances, flying toward the river in full gallop, would never see it.

Ian was in deadly fear. Her horse, hearing the sound of drumming hoofs behind, stretched himself even further. In desperation Ian turned off onto a small path that bypassed the main road. With his head down on his horse's neck to keep him from being swept off he plunged through the undergrowth and then swung out onto the main road, positioning his horse across it so Frances had to stop. She pulled up, rocking a little in the saddle from the suddenness. He leaned forward toward her and struck her, openhanded, across her left cheek. Her horse reared a little in fright.

"You deserved that," Ian said, his voice shaking. "You damn little fool, the bridge is washed out."

She looked from his taut face to the swollen river, the bridge, and the small sign. Her eyes widened and then slowly swung back to his face. At this moment the heavens opened and the rain poured down.

"Come on," Ian said through shut teeth. "There's a cottage just down this road." He turned his horse's head and, obediently, she fell in beside him. Neither of them spoke as they cantered toward the small, thatched-roof cottage he had pointed out.

The overhanging trees provided some cover but the rain was hard and they were both thoroughly drenched by the time they reached the shelter of the cottage. It was empty so Ian forced the door and let Frances in while he went to put the horses in the shed.

The cottage was clearly someone's home. There was rough but comfortable furniture in the main room and wood stacked neatly by the fireplace. When Ian came in, blinking drops off his lashes, Frances was competently building a fire. It flared up as she lit it, illuminating her rain-wet figure and tumbling hair. She raised her arms to push it off her face and turned to look at him. He crossed the room to stand beside her. The mark of his hand was still on her cheek. He reached out to touch it.

"I didn't mean to hit you, mo chridhe," he said, and

57

he spoke in Gaelic. "You frightened me." A strand of her wet hair caught on his fingers. He looked at the pale gold tendril, then back to her face. He regarded her unsmiling for what seemed to her a very long time. Her heart was hammering in her breast. He left the fire and went over to the old sofa and picked up the blanket that was neatly folded across its back. Then he returned to the hearth and spread it on the floor.

"What are you going to do?" she asked in the same language he had spoken in. They were the first words she had spoken since he struck her.

"Make love to you, m'eudail." He took a step toward her and, instinctively, she moved backwards. He stopped dead. "Frances." His voice was very deep and she stared as if hypnotized into the darkness of his eyes. "Come here," he said softly.

There were three steps between them. In the five seconds before she took those steps Frances made a decision. Then she moved and he reached out and caught her against him, his mouth coming down hard on her own. She slid her hands under the wetness of his coat and held him close. She could feel the strong muscles of his back under her palms. He did not release her mouth as he swung her into his arms and then knelt to lay her on the blanket. Frances opened her eyes to look up into his passion-hard face. His hands were on the buttons of her shirt and then she felt his lips on her breast. As she closed her eyes and gave herself to the growing urgency of his passion, the thought that lay behind her surrender flickered once again through her mind. He won't leave me now.

*   *   *

They lay close together for some time without speaking then Frances said softly ''Ian?''

''Hmn?'' he raised himself on an elbow to look down at her face, framed by the primitive splendor of her ash-blond hair. There was a very faint mark on her cheek. He bent to kiss it.

''You've been doing this with someone else,'' she said in accusation.

''What?'' He stared at her in astonishment.

''I'm not a fool,'' she said heatedly. ''I can tell. Who is she?''

He flopped back onto the blanket, his face vivid with amusement. ''Frances, I love you. You never say the expected thing.''

She frowned suspiciously. ''What expected thing?''

''Something tender,'' he said, laughter trembling in his voice. ''Think of all the tender things I've just been saying to you.''

''The point is, who else have you been saying them to?'' she said inexorably.

''No one.'' He was positive. ''Stop being so silly.''

She sat up and stared at him. ''Silly?'' she said. ''*I* haven't been making love to other people.''

The amusement abruptly left his face. ''You'd better not.''

''What would you do if you found out I was?'' she asked curiously.

''Kill him and beat you,'' he replied promptly.

She seemed to find this answer satisfactory, because she pillowed her head on his shoulder. He felt her long lashes sweep against his skin as she closed her eyes. ''We should leave,'' she sighed.

The rain beat hard against the window. ''We can't,''

he said with conviction. "It's raining." His hands moved over her body with exquisite precision. After a moment she yielded to his caresses, with a quiver that ignited his passion to fever pitch. When she lay in his arms, afterwards, utterly still, utterly his, she understood too with a woman's powerful knowledge that in some profound way she had also possessed him.

When the rain stopped they rode back to Wick. They did not discuss the future. Neither of them wanted, at that moment, to spoil the magic of the present.

Chapter Eight

And fare thee well, my only luve,
   And fare thee well a while.
And I will come again, my luve,
   Tho' it were ten thousand mile!

                    —ROBERT BURNS

There were a few suspiciously raised eyebrows when Frances and Ian arrived back at Wick, together, dishevelled, and late for dinner. They were laughingly casual about being caught in the rainstorm, but Lady Mary Graham was not at all pleased with what had happened. "This is precisely the sort of behavior that can ruin a girl's reputation," she scolded her niece. "Really, I am quite annoyed at Lady Darlington for allowing you to fall behind like that. And you, too, Frances. You ought to know better. People have such nasty minds. There is bound to be someone ready to think the worst of you."

They wouldn't be far wrong, thought Frances with a flash of amusement. But she meekly bowed her head and listened to her aunt's strictures with sweet docility. Her thoughts were elsewhere.

After dinner that evening the whole company assembled around the piano in the drawing room. Lady Darlington urged her daughter to play, which she did very prettily. Catherine was an attractive girl and she showed to advantage at the piano, a fact of which her mother was very aware. Then another young lady played a very competent Mozart sonata. "Won't you honor us with your talents, Miss Stewart?" asked Lady Darlington, honor-bound to include Frances in the entertainment.

The others chorused their similar wishes with varying degrees of enthusiasm, and Frances's eyes went once again to the magnet that had drawn them all evening. Ian smiled at her very faintly and she said slowly, "All right." She crossed to the piano and sat down, her face looking grave and abstracted. "This is a Scottish ballad about a girl who loved a boy called Geordie," she said simply, and, striking a few notes, she began to sing. The song had all the power of the great ballads and her voice was marvelous: deep and clear and perfectly controlled. As the last note died away there was a sigh in the room, as if a great collective breath had been let out. The faintest, briefest glint of recognition showed in Frances's eyes, and then she sang another. When she had finished and started to get up Robert Sedburgh said quietly, "You would please us all if you would sing one more, Miss Stewart." She looked back at him, smiled suddenly, and said,

"Very well, I'll do something different—something in Gaelic. This is a victory song of the clans. It should, of course, be played on the pipes." But the wild, triumphant cry of the bagpipes was echoed in her voice as she launched into the exultant war cry of the Macdonalds of Lochaber.

Ian's face blazed as he listened to the fierce Gaelic words calling out the traditional invitation to the wolves of Lochaber to come feast on the flesh of the fallen enemy. The rest of the company did not understand the words, but the spirit was unmistakable. It was not civilized, Robert Sedburgh thought as he watched Ian Macdonald's face, but it was magnificent.

When Frances finally rose from the piano her eyes met Ian's in a glance of such unvoiced intensity that Robert Sedburgh was shocked. Something *had* happened this afternoon; he was almost sure of it. Lord Robert loved Frances very much and his antennae were extremely sensitive where she was concerned. He observed her closely for the rest of the evening, and he did not like what he saw.

The incident that disturbed him most occurred toward the end of the evening. He and Ian were standing talking by the tall French windows. Lady Darlington had finished pouring tea and Frances was seated on a sofa next to Catherine Darlington, still holding her cup and talking about music. Lord Robert said something to Ian and Ian agreed, put his plate down and suddenly yawned. "I beg your pardon," he apologized easily. "I have been somewhat short of sleep these last few days."

"Perhaps you ought to seek your bed early this evening," said Lord Robert courteously.

Ian nodded agreement, looked at Frances's back with warm and peaceful eyes, and smiled faintly. She turned around as if he had touched her.

It was defeat for Robert Sedburgh and he knew it. The rest of the night his face wore an uncharacteristically harsh expression that was underlined by the unhappiness in his eyes whenever he looked at Frances.

*   *   *

The next day Lady Mary Graham received a letter from her sister which caused her to pack her bags and her niece and depart abruptly for Somerset. Mrs. Treveleyn had had a miscarriage and urgently needed the solace of Lady Mary's company, so wrote Mr. Treveleyn, Lady Mary's brother-in-law. Frances did not want to go, but in the face of her aunt's real distress she made no complaint. She went to Somerset, was helpful when she could be, and kept out of the way when she couldn't. They stayed three weeks.

They arrived back in London on September 8. On September 9 Ian called. Frances took him to the room Douglas was using as a studio on the pretense of showing him her portrait. Lady Mary let them go. Whatever was between Frances and Ian wouldn't go away by keeping them apart and she had come to the conclusion that they had better make a decision one way or another. So she refrained from accompanying them, for which Frances gave her a grateful smile.

Ian did look at the picture. It was almost finished; Douglas was working on background at present. Ian's gaze went from the radiant young face of the portrait to the girl beside him. "Anyone who didn't know you would say Douglas was a liar," he said soberly.

Faint color stained her cheeks. He so rarely complimented her. "I think it's good," she admitted.

"It looks like you," he said laconically. He turned away, dismissing the portrait from his mind in favor of the model. "God, I didn't think you were ever coming back."

"Neither did I."

His eyes on her were intent. "Shall I speak to your uncle?"

She smiled at him, a glowing vital smile that illuminated her face. "Yes. I heard from Papa. He says you will have no trouble enrolling in the University of Edinburgh. We can live with him and . . ."

He listened to her run on, a look of incredulity growing on his face. Finally he cut in harshly. "You really don't expect me to go back to school?"

The light died from her face to be replaced by a braced and wary stillness. "If you don't return to school," she finally answered, "how do you intend to earn a living? My money from my mother isn't enough to live on."

All the muscles in Ian's face hardened. "I'll go into the army, of course."

"Then don't bother to speak to my uncle," she returned with ominous calm. "I won't marry you."

"Frances! You don't mean that."

"I do."

And there it was. He looked at the slender loveliness in front of him. He could snap her in two with his hands, but he could not break her will. It was a granite wall, firm, categorical, unassailable. He tried once more. "You may have to marry me."

Her eyes were grass green. "No, I won't," she lied determinedly. "I am all right."

Ian fought to get a grip on his anger. He wanted to shake her. Worse, he wanted to throw her down . . . Frances correctly read the look in his eyes and stepped backwards. She knew that terrifying temper. "Don't touch me," she said breathlessly.

A mask of control came down over his features,

almost but not quite hiding the passion beneath. "I have no intention of touching you," he said coldly. "I will give you a warning, though, Frances. This is the last time I'll ask you to marry me. You won't get a chance to change your mind."

Her face suddenly blazed. "Go marry the army!" she shouted, as angry now as he. "That's your true love."

He stared at her for a few silent moments and a nerve quivered in his cheek. "Goodbye," he finally said in the same cold voice as before. He crossed the room and went out, shutting the door behind him. Outside he paused for a minute, his head bent; there was no sound from within. He straightened and walked quickly down the hall, his stride long and even as usual.

Frances listened to him go. "He'll be back," she said to her portrait as the sound of his steps died away. "I know he will."

After he left Frances Ian went directly to the house of Andrés Bello, where he was fortunate enough to find Simón Bolívar. They had a long and serious conversation. The next day, when Colonel Bolívar sailed for South America in a British man-of-war, Ian Macdonald was with him.

It was left to Douglas to break the news to Frances. He had not had an opportunity to talk to Ian. There had been a letter for him at the breakfast table yesterday morning and one for Ian's mother. In his letter to Douglas Ian had spelled out his reasons for accompanying Bolívar. "I have spoken to Colonel Bolívar at length," he wrote. "There are many things about the situation in South America that I do not understand, but I do recog-

66

nize in the desire for independence a state of affairs worth fighting for. And Bolívar is, I believe, a great man. He will be to South America what Washington was to the United States. The opportunity to join an enterprise of such magnitude is irresistible.'' He mentioned Frances only indirectly, in his concluding remark. ''After all, there is nothing for me at home.''

So now Douglas had to face her, and he was not looking forward to the task. He asked to see Lady Mary first and briefly explained his mission to her. She sent for Frances to come to the drawing room and, after an anxious look at her niece, left the room. ''Mr. Macdonald has some news for you, my dear,'' she said softly. ''If you want me I will be in the morning parlor.''

Douglas was left alone with Frances. He had worried all day yesterday about this encounter. It was the first time, so far as he knew, that Frances had not gotten her way. He did not know how she would react; Frances, under the sweet serenity she pretended to the world, had a temper almost as dangerous as Ian's. Douglas, who had watched and loved her for years, was one of the few to realize that.

''What is the matter, Douglas?'' She looked pale but composed.

''Frances.'' It had to be said. ''Frances, Ian has gone to South America with Colonel Bolívar. He sailed yesterday.''

''What?'' Her long green eyes stared uncomprehendingly at Douglas's concerned face. ''South America?''

''Venezuela, to be precise. Caracas has declared its independence from Spain. There is bound to be fighting. General Miranda has gone as well, to command the South American troops.''

"South America," she said again, slowly this time. She felt bitterness surge through her heart. Never, it seemed to her, would she forgive him for this. She stood still, with a hard, frozen face, and let Douglas's words wash over her. Finally a phrase of his penetrated her consciousness. "What did you say?" she asked.

"I said that one of the reasons he went was because, as he put it, 'there is nothing for me at home.' "

There was a blank silence and then Frances blindly raised her hands toward him. He moved quickly to take her in his arms, feeling her hold to him fiercely as the sobs of deep, terrible grief shook her. "It will be all right," he found himself saying. "He will come back." But she sobbed on and refused to be comforted.

Chapter Nine

O how can I be blithe and glad,
   Or how can I gang brisk and braw,
When the bonnie lad that I lo'e best
   Is o'er the hills and far away?
—ROBERT BURNS

Robert Sedburgh had gone home to Aysgarth after he left Wick, and when he returned to London a month later it was with the thought of reporting to the Horse Guards that he was ready to return to Portugal. The news that Ian Macdonald had left for South America sent him round to Hanover Square in a hurry. For the first time in a month hope flickered in his heart. He had been so sure she was going to marry Macdonald.

He found Frances sitting with her aunt in the drawing room. She looked pale but she smiled when she saw him and asked him to be seated. "What does Frances Stewart look like?" his mother had asked curiously, having heard reports from his aunts in London. As he looked now at the blonde head of the girl before him he mentally shook his head. There was no describing Frances.

She talked with him calmly and amusingly and said yes, she was going to Mrs. Carstairs's ball that evening and yes, she would save a dance for him. As he left his brow was faintly puckered. On the surface she seemed the same, but the springing vitality he had so loved was gone. He had never seen her so subdued.

He watched her carefully for a week and then, having prepared Lady Mary, he called in Hanover Square and was allowed to see her alone. "I asked you a question some months ago, Miss Stewart," he said steadily. "You begged me at the time not to pressure you for an immediate answer. I have obeyed your wishes but I have not forgotten. Do you feel it possible to answer me now?"

She refused to meet his eyes. "I cannot marry you, my lord," she said in a voice so low he could barely hear it.

Lord Robert had been a very good soldier. He decided it was time to go on the attack. "Why not?" he asked unexpectedly.

She moved restlessly to the window with her lithe long walk. She fingered the velvet drapes. "Because I don't love you."

"I love you," he answered quietly. "Don't you think, perhaps, you might learn to love me in return? I can be very persuasive."

At last she looked at him. His blue eyes were tender as they rested on her troubled face. It was the tenderness that broke her. She bent her head and he saw the heavy tears falling on her hands as she held to the velvet drapery. "Frances!" He crossed the room swiftly to stand beside her and she raised her tear-streaked face to his.

"I can't marry you, my lord," she repeated. "I can't marry anyone. Not now."

"Not now." At those words a vivid picture flashed in his mind, of Ian touching Frances with a smile. His voice was uncharacteristically rough as he asked, "What did he do to you?"

Her eyes widened until they were great liquid pools of green. He was standing over her so that his shoulders blotted out the rest of the room, but his aspect was not at all menacing. Rather, it was strangely comforting. He was on her side, Frances thought confusedly. And because she was frightened and didn't know what to do, she told him. "I'm going to have a baby."

He felt as if someone had hit him across the face without provocation or warning. "My God!" he said, and she bowed her head again. "Macdonald's?" he asked shortly, and the golden head nodded.

Lord Robert's blue eyes were black with anger. "And he left you?" he asked incredulously.

"He didn't know," her voice was muffled. She went on, automatically coming to Ian's defense, "He asked me. I said I was all right."

"But why?"

She couldn't tell him the real reason. "I was angry," she said. She was as still now as she had been restless before. She raised her beautiful eyes to his and said, "I don't know what I'm going to do."

He stared down at her, and there was a white line around his mouth. "I said once there was nothing I wouldn't do for you," he said at last. "I meant it. Marry me."

She looked pale as a waxen saint. "I can't do that."

His mouth twisted. "Do you find me so repulsive?"

"No!" There was distress in her voice. "Of course not. Only there is more involved here than just the two of us. You are a man of great position. You cannot accept another man's son as your heir."

"The child may be a girl," he said steadily. "I'll take the chance." He smiled somewhat crookedly. "Don't think me a hero, Frances. I thought I had lost you. If this is the only way I can get you, I'll take it. If we are married immediately no one will ever know the child isn't mine."

She looked searchingly into his face. What she saw there seemed to reassure her. "Are you certain?" she said hesitantly.

He had not yet touched her. He put his hands on her shoulders now and felt her stiffen slightly. A sudden fear struck him. His love for Frances was not at all brotherly. With sudden decision he pulled her closer, bending his head to find her lips.

His mouth was warm and hard and insistent on hers and Frances instinctively resisted him. But then she opened her eyes and saw his face, the bright hair falling forward over his forehead. He was not at all like Ian. Slowly her heart quieted and she leaned against him, comforted by his strong arms and slow-moving kisses. When he finally raised his head his blue eyes looked relieved. "It's going to be all right," he said in a rich, deep voice.

"Yes," she replied on a note of wonder. "I think it is."

They were married a week later and Robert took her first to the lakes and then home to Aysgarth. His father and mother were pleased to learn that their son had

72

carried off the girl who was being called the beauty of the century, and soon they came to appreciate Frances for her own sake. They were both gentle and kind, reasonable and satisfied. The house itself was very lovely, with huge rooms furnished with sixteenth-, seventeenth-, and eighteenth-century furniture. It was the sort of house that had grown gradually, under centuries of Sedburgh guardianship. Frances, who was used to Scottish country houses, products of colder winters and families with considerably less money than the Sedburghs, was very impressed. The first time she had seen it it had seemed enormous and powerful and intimidating, but it was the kind of household that was still rooted in its neighborhood, and she soon found that while the scale of life was different from what she was used to, the substance was not.

Robert's three younger brothers were at school, so the Earl and Countess of Aysgarth were the only other inhabitants of the house for most of the time. When it became obvious that Frances was going to have a child they were delighted. Lady Aysgarth spent hours telling Frances about the history of the Sedburgh family, which had acquired its earldom under Elizabeth.

Frances was wretched. She had lied to everyone about the expected date of birth and no one seemed to doubt her word. She was tall and carried well; it never seemed to occur to anyone that she was two months more pregnant than she had said she was. It was not fear of discovery that made her so miserable. It was the deception itself. The more she heard about the ancient lineage of the Sedburgh family, the more she saw of their quality, the more profoundly unhappy she became. When she brought her trouble up to Robert he had tried to be reassuring. "If the baby is a boy, he will be my son. That is all there is to it, Frances. He will be brought up here at Aysgarth and he will learn to love it as well as any Sedburgh. Don't worry."

But, of course, she did worry. He made light of her concern but it was not a light matter. She knew that and he knew it as well. She prayed night and day to the Holy Virgin that her baby would be a girl.

On May 7 Frances's maid came into her bedroom to find her lying on the floor. She had been rearranging some flowers, had stepped back to regard them, tripped over a small stool, fallen, and hit her head on the corner of a table. She had knocked herself out. The maid shrieked for help and Robert, who was coming up the stairs, ran into the room. Frances was just stirring. White-lipped with fear he had carried her to the bed and sent for the doctor. Aside from a painful bruise on her temple, she was pronounced to be all right. The doctor recommended a good night's sleep.

Her labor pains began early the following morning. She went through the connecting door into Robert's room and woke him. At the touch of her hand on his arm he sat up immediately. "The pains have started, Rob," she said quietly. "I think you'd better send for the doctor."

He swung himself out of bed and put a supporting arm around her. "Let me put you back into bed first." As they returned slowly to her room he said calmly, "Frances, it was the fall. That's why the baby is early."

Her eyes looked enormous in her pale face. "Yes," she said. "I hadn't thought of that." Her hand tightened for a minute on his arm. "Rob, I'm so frightened."

He knew it wasn't childbirth that terrified her but the

result of it. "It will be all right," he said soothingly. "Even if it's a boy and the spitting image of Macdonald we'll brazen it out together. Now let me help you into bed and I'll ring for your maid."

For a brief moment her lips rested against his hand. "You're so good to me."

"Of course I am," he replied reasonably. "I love you. Now for God's sake will you get into bed! It's freezing out here!" And with a shaken laugh she obeyed.

Frances's daughter was born six hours later. She was six pounds, a very decent weight for a seven-month baby. She had downy hair and her eyes were blue. Frances took one look at her and tears of relief and tenderness slid down her face. "She's beautiful," she whispered.

Robert was staring, fascinated. "She's so tiny." Gently he touched the baby's fingers and the infant looked at him, a corner of its mouth flaring up. "She smiled at me!" He sounded genuinely delighted. Frances looked at him.

"I don't deserve you, Rob," she said humbly.

"Maybe not," he grinned at her, "but you've got me. Forever."

Chapter Ten

If love for love thou wilt na gie
At least be pity to me shown

—ROBERT BURNS

Eighteen months later Lord Robert Sedburgh, his wife, and his daughter paid a rare visit to London. The occasion was an exhibit by Douglas Macdonald at the Royal Academy. Frances had been delighted when she heard the news from Douglas and had immediately asked Robert if they could go up to London to see it. He had not really wanted to go; he had repeatedly found reasons why a stay in London would be impossible. But now he looked at the eager face of his wife and relented. This time, he could see, she really wanted to go. At the last minute Lady Aysgarth had not felt well and so they brought the baby, who had been named Helen after Frances's mother, with them.

The Earl of Aysgarth had a house in Berkeley Square which he had opened and staffed for the use of his son and daughter-in-law. They planned to stay for at least a month. It was not London that Robert had been avoiding for all these months but the Macdonalds, specifically Douglas and Charlie. He did not care to have Frances reminded of Ian. However, it was inevitable that they meet at some time, he realized, and so he was the one who proposed the longer visit.

They had been in town for two days when Frances wrote to tell Douglas they had arrived. He came immediately. She heard his voice as she was coming down the main stairs and went herself into the front hall to welcome him. "Douglas! How marvelous to see you. We're so excited about your exhibition. Come into the drawing room and tell me about it." She drew his arm through hers and began to walk him down the hall. Over her shoulder she said to the butler, "Bring some sherry, Matthews."

Douglas was regarding her with an expression that Frances barely noticed, she was so accustomed to seeing it in the eyes of men when they looked at her. She smiled warmly and sat down. "Tell me all about it," she repeated. "I made Robert bring me to London as soon as I heard. Imagine. The Royal Academy!"

Douglas blinked and abruptly sat down. After a moment's silence he began to do as she requested. When he had finished the tale and had promised to escort them himself to see the paintings he asked courteously, "But how is the baby, Frances? She must be walking by now."

Frances grinned. "She's been walking for eight months, Douglas! And she's fine. You can see for yourself. We brought her with us." She rang the bell.

Douglas smiled a little painfully. "Oh, good."

The butler came in. "Matthews, will you ask Nurse to bring Miss Helen down to the drawing room, please?"

"Yes, my lady." The butler nodded magisterially and withdrew. In ten minutes a stout middle-aged woman appeared holding a little girl by the hand.

"Thank you, Nurse," Frances said. "I'll bring her back to the nursery later." The little girl ran to Frances and immediately climbed up into her lap, staring with huge gray eyes at the strange man sitting in her mother's drawing room.

"This is Mr. Macdonald, Nell," Frances said. "He is a good friend of Mama's. Will you say hello?"

"Hello," the little girl said gravely, staring at Douglas with the relentless gaze of childhood. She was a beautiful child. She had hair of dark gold and eyes the deep gray of a northern loch.

"Hello, Nell," Douglas replied equally solemnly. "I am very glad to meet you."

Nell considered this in silence for a few minutes, then got off Frances's lap and went over to him. "What that?"

Douglas looked ruefully at his finger. "A paint stain," he admitted. "I like to paint, Nell." Nell looked incredulous and he smiled. "I know it isn't a very grown-up thing to do but I like it."

The child's eye was caught by an ornament on a table over on the far side of the room and she toddled toward it determinedly. "She looks like your father, Frances," he said.

"Yes," she agreed. "So everyone says." Nell had reached the ornament. She picked it up.

"Mama!" she said excitedly. "A horsie!"

"Yes, love, I see. Bring it here carefully and we'll look at it." Frances smiled at the child who grinned back, her small face lighting up in a way that made her suddenly resemble unmistakably the man who was her father.

Douglas's breath rasped in his throat. Frances was still smiling lovingly at Nell, who was coming toward her carefully holding the horse. She turned briefly to say something to Douglas and when she saw the appalled recognition in his eyes her own face sobered. "Is it as obvious as that?", she asked out of a constricted throat.

He looked from the child to her. "No," he said after a minute. "She really doesn't look like him at all. It's the smile."

Her face never changed. "I know."

"Only someone who knew him very well would ever see it." For some reason he couldn't bring himself to say Ian's name. "God, Frances! I had no idea."

"Thank you, sweetie," she said to her daughter. "Yes, look at his mane and his tail. Just like a real horse. Sit down here and you can play with him. It's bronze," she said to Douglas as if answering a question of his. "It won't break."

"Frances!"

"Yes?" She spoke almost absently.

"Does Robert know?" He was surprised to see a flame of anger in her eyes.

"What do you take me for, Douglas? Of course he knows. He married me anyway."

Douglas stared at her for a minute and then his mouth took on a grim look. "Of course," he said, "I asked the wrong question. I should have asked does Ian know?"

Her eyes fell away from his to rest on the bright curls of her daughter. "No," she said shortly. "And I don't want him to know."

"Why did you let him go, Frances?" His eyes too were on the child, playing so happily with her new find.

To Douglas she told the truth. "Because I wanted him to stay for me. Not for anything else. Just for me."

He nodded slowly as if her answer made perfect sense, as, to him, it did. "He is still in South America," he volunteered, giving her the information she longed for but would never ask for. "I wrote, of course, to tell him about your marriage. I hear from him periodically."

"I understand that the republicans were badly beaten," she said in a stiff voice.

He stared at her in surprise. He had never before known Frances to concern herself about foreign affairs, and the news from Venezuela was hardly easily come by. "Yes," he said. "Bolívar is presently in New Granada, in Cartagena to be precise. Ian is with him. They are determined to convince New Granada to assist them in a new effort to liberate Venezuela."

Frances's face was shadowed. "I see," she said quietly.

There was the sound of a step in the hall, and the door opened. "Papa!" Nell cried, her face vivid with joy. She ran toward Robert Sedburgh, her arms held out.

"Nell!" the tall blond man laughed back and swung her up into his arms. "How is my girl?"

She giggled delightedly as he held her over his head; then he sat her in the crook of his arm and crossed the room. Frances watched him come, her eyes warm with tenderness. "Rob, you remember Douglas Macdonald," she said.

"Of course." He put Nell down and went to shake hands with Douglas. "We are looking forward to seeing your exhibit," he said courteously. "In fact, it is the main reason for our visit to London."

"I am flattered," returned Douglas. "And very pleased."

Robert sat down and Nell immediately climbed up his legs, clutching her horse. "Look, Papa!" she said urgently. He bent his head to the child and Frances said mournfully, "Deserted again."

Robert laughed at her. "You're an old story," he said. "I'm a treat."

But she shook her head. "Nell has been Papa's girl virtually since she was born," she explained to Douglas. "She only puts up with me until she can get her hands on him. She's a true female, I'm afraid." At this point a very serious look descended over Nell's face. "Oh dear," said Frances comically, jumping up. "I think it's time to remove her upstairs. I know that look."

Robert handed her over with alacrity. "By all means," he said definitely, and both he and Douglas watched as she carried the little girl out of the room. Then Robert turned to Douglas. He had not missed the shadow on Frances's face when he came in.

"Frances looks well," Douglas said. He hesitated. "She looks happy," he added finally.

"I think she is." Robert's blue eyes stared at Douglas with a straight, uncompromising look. "Were you talking to her about Macdonald?" he asked steadily.

Douglas, thrown off balance by such a direct approach, answered truthfully. "Yes."

The clear blue gaze kindled. "I thought so. She didn't look happy when I came in the door." He leaned forward in his chair. "The less Frances hears about or is reminded of him the better it will be for her. I don't want her upset. She is my wife and I can keep her safe and happy so long as he stays away. He is still in South America I take it."

"Yes," said Douglas briefly.

"He would do himself no good by coming back."

"I think he knows that." Douglas rose. "You have nothing to worry about, Lord Robert. Frances is, as you said, your wife. That is not a commitment she would ever take lightly."

After Douglas had left Robert sat still staring into the fire with a preoccupied face. He looked like a man wrestling with a major problem.

The Sedburghs went to the theater that night. Their box was besieged at the intermissions. Robert could scarcely see his wife for the masculine heads clustered around her.

"You're a lucky dog, Rob," said Henry Farringdon in his ear. "For the past two years I've been telling myself that nobody could be as beautiful as I remembered Frances Stewart. And now here she is, and my memory seems dull in comparison."

Robert looked at him almost remotely. "Yes," he said. "And how have you been, Henry?"

Their conversation was halted by Frances, who had risen and come across to them. "Good evening, Lady Robert," said Mr. Farringdon reverently. She gave him her hand and Robert said, "London must have been dull without you, my love."

She cast him a glance of amusement mingled with irritation. "I think the next act is about to start," she said pointedly and they finally managed to clear out their box.

Frances's maid was brushing her hair that evening when the connecting door between their bedrooms opened and Robert came in. He was still in his evening shirt, which he had opened at the neck. He sat down in a rose velvet chair, leaned back, and regarded his wife thoughtfully.

The maid was vigorously pulling the brush through her thick hair, which glistened in the firelight. She wore a green velvet robe the color of her eyes. She looked at Robert in the mirror and said to her maid, "That will be all, Mary, thank you. You may go to bed now."

"Yes, my lady." The maid discreetly retired, closing the bedroom door quietly behind her.

Frances smiled at her husband. "A busy day," she said lightly.

He did not smile back. "Yes," he agreed. "It was." She didn't say anything and after a moment he went on, "I think half of London has remained bachelors because of you."

She regarded him steadily. "Is that what is bothering you, Rob?"

"No," he said. "I'm not such a fool as to be jealous of your popularity." There was a note of anger in his voice and, hearing it, she rose and went to stand at the foot of the bed so that she was directly facing him.

"Then what is the matter?" she asked quietly. "You've been strange all evening."

"Have I?" he laughed harshly. Then, as if the words were wrenched out of him against his will, he brought it out. "Tell me, Frances, what would you do if Ian Macdonald came back?"

"What would I do?" She stared at him in amazement. "Good God, Rob, you don't think I'd betray you? After all you've done . . ."

He swore, something he never did. "I don't want you to stay with me out of gratitude!" The note of anger she had heard in his voice a moment before had reappeared, and mixed with it now was an audible strain of bitterness.

Frances was deadly serious. She had never seen him like this before and she was suddenly certain that the whole future of her marriage depended on how she handled this moment. Her eyes flickered quickly to the bed beside her. He saw the look. "Oh, I have no right to complain. I know that. You've never refused me. You're always warm and loving." He stood up and went to poke at the fire. "Forget what I said." He leaned his shoulders against the mantel and looked at her still composure out of eyes that were wary and guarded against hurt.

"I can't forget it," she said. Robert was right. This was not a problem that could be settled by going to bed. It required words. The right words. From her. She took a breath and said to him what she had never said before. "How could I leave you, Rob? I love you."

The sudden harsh intake of his breath betrayed him. He took an involuntary step toward her and then stopped. "You don't have to say that."

"I said it because I wanted to say it and because it is the truth. I love you." She grinned at him mischievously. "Now what are you going to do about it?"

"I'll think of something," he answered, his own face lighting in a returning smile as he crossed the room purposefully and scooped her up into his arms.

Chapter Eleven

> O lang will his ladie
> Look frae the Castle Doune,
> Ere she see the Earl o' Moray
> Come soondan throu the toun
>
> —Anonymous

Douglas heard nothing from Frances for six months after she had returned to Aysgarth. They had always corresponded intermittently but now even that communication was severed. Frances, aware for the first time of Robert's insecurity, did not want to do anything to feed it. And Douglas understood that Robert wanted to see her relationship with the Macdonalds broken. With his uncomfortable facility for seeing the other person's point of view, Douglas could not say he blamed him.

Consequently, Douglas was stunned to receive a brief message from Frances in August. Her characteristically firm handwriting looked strangely uneven. "Robert has been killed," she wrote. "Can you come? Frances."

Five hours later he was in Kent, turning into the Aysgarth drive. The butler showed him into a large, beautifully paneled room and said, "I will inform Lady Robert you have arrived, sir."

Douglas nodded, then frowned and said, "Wait! Can you tell me what happened—it is Coombs, is it not?"

"Yes, sir," said Coombs. The man's face was furrowed with sorrow. "It was a fall from a horse, Mr. Macdonald. Lord Robert was returning from an inspection of the new cottage repairs. From what we've been told he was cantering along the woodland path when a child darted out onto the path directly in front of him. He pulled his horse up so abruptly that the horse lost its balance and fell to its knees. Lord Robert was thrown. He hit his head on a rock." The butler's voice began to tremble. "He never regained consciousness, Mr. Macdonald. The mother of the child saw what had happened and fetched help. They brought him back to Aysgarth and he died three hours later in Lady Robert's arms."

"Oh my dear God," Douglas was shaken to the core. "Thank you, Coombs."

"Yes, sir." The servant looked directly at him and the class barrier between them crumbled. "I'm glad you've come, Mr. Macdonald. Lord and Lady Aysgarth are distraught and Miss Helen is frightened and bewildered. Lady Robert needs someone to stand by her."

"That I can do, Coombs," Douglas returned. "I only wish I could do more."

When Frances came into the saloon a few minutes later Douglas thought his heart would break looking at her. She wore a soft black dress and her hair was combed smoothly off her face and fastened in a loose knot at the nape of her neck. She was very pale. "Douglas!" Her voice broke. "I'm so glad you've come."

"Oh, my dear," he said, his voice infinitely gentle. "I am so sorry." He held out his arms and for the second time in his life felt the slender, grief-stricken body of his only love sobbing against his shoulder.

"I'm sorry, Douglas," she finally said, the words muffled by his coat. "I always seem to be crying on you." He didn't reply, but very briefly he allowed his cheek to touch her hair. She drew back and dried her cheeks with a lacy handkerchief. "I still can't believe it. We were going to Cornwall next week, just the two of us. It was going to be another honeymoon, Rob said." Abruptly she stopped talking and bit her lip.

"I came immediately," he said. "Thank God I was in London."

"Papa could not get here in time for the funeral, you see," she explained. "It's set for tomorrow. And I needed someone of mine. Thank you, Douglas, for coming."

Later that night as he lay in bed listening to the rustle of the trees outside his window, Douglas thought about her words. "Someone of mine . . ." That was how she regarded him. A big brother. A faithful friend. Someone of hers. It never crossed her mind that his feelings for her were stronger than hers for him. She never cast enough thought his way to think it was a painful role for him to act as a brother to her whom he had loved since first he set eyes on her. Her pale, sorrowful face with its great sad eyes stirred and moved him just as the flowerlike child's face had so many years ago at Castle Hunter. She was his love, although she never thought of him. He would walk over burning coals for her sake. And she would never know how much it cost him.

Lord Robert Sedburgh was buried the next day, a day of beautiful August weather that seemed to mock the somberness of the occasion. For the first time Frances entered the little gray stone church where the Sedburghs had worshipped for centuries. The service instead of comforting her filled her with a greater sense of desolation. It seemed intolerable that she had to say goodbye to Rob in this alien church, in this alien service. She missed, achingly, the plangent tolling of Gregorian chant, the rich sound of the Latin rite. Yet this was Rob's church. It was the service he would have wanted. He seemed very far away from her now.

That evening after a dinner full of long silences, Lady Aysgarth announced she was going to bed, and Frances drifted into the drawing room and over to the piano. Robert's mother on the stairs heard the first few notes and turned to go back. Frances shouldn't be playing the piano now, she thought. Then she stopped as Frances began to sing. It was an old ballad, but neither Lady Aysgarth nor the two men listening in the dining room had ever heard it sung like that; slow and measured and full of grief, like the role of a muffled drum:

> Ye Highlands and ye Lawlands
>   O where hae ye been?
> They hae slain the Earl o' Moray
>   And laid him on the green.
>
> He was a braw gallant
>   And he rid at the ring
> And the bonny Earl o' Moray
>   O he may hae been a king!

> O lang will his ladie
> Look frae the Castle Doune,
> Ere she see the Earl o' Moray
> Come soondan throu the toun.

The last note died away and Lady Aysgarth turned back up the stairs, the tears sliding silently down her face. In the dining room Douglas sat with bowed head, listening to words that were written about the death of a sixteenth-century Stewart noble sung now by another Stewart for the untimely death of another fine young man. Lord Aysgarth said to him, "I shall always be glad that Robert had Frances, even if only for a little while. He loved her so."

"Yes," said Douglas, staring at the tablecloth. "I know he did."

Douglas stayed until Frances's father came and then he left for London. He found a letter from Ian awaiting him. It was a long letter, full of news of the South American campaign. New Granada had agreed to assist Bolívar in a new effort to free Venezuela from the iron rule of Monteverde, the irregular naval officer who was ruling in the name of the royalists. In order to counter Monteverde's brutal tactics of killing out of hand any and all republicans he could find, Bolívar had responded with a proclamation of *guerra a muerte*—"war to the death." No longer, Ian wrote, would quarter be given to captured royalists.

"I do not think myself that it is a good idea," he wrote, "although I can understand why Bolívar was forced to do it. Too many Venezuelans are serving with

91

the royalists because they know that if we capture them they will be spared whereas if they were republicans and captured they would be killed out of hand. As a result of *guerra a muerte* we may get more volunteers, but I don't think the resulting bloodbath will be worth it. Bolívar wants to found a homeland and so it is in his interest to increase the population and wealth of Venezuela. He is defeating his own purposes by this action.

"But, God, Douglas, he is a great man! Here he was at Trujillo, with six hundred men behind him, declaring war on the whole Spanish Empire. One can't help but love a man like that."

At the very end of the letter, as though it was an afterthought, he wrote, "How is Frances?"

Douglas replied almost immediately with the news of Robert's death. He sent the letter to Caracas. How, he wondered, did one deliver mail to a man in the middle of a *guerra a muerte*?

Ten months after Robert's death Frances went to live with her father in Edinburgh. Robert's brother John was finished with Oxford and living at home and it was obvious to everyone, his parents included, that he was much more devoted to Frances than he should be. When Frances had told Lady Aysgarth she was going to go to her father, the countess had reluctantly agreed it would be best. Frances had promised to bring Nell to London for a visit twice a year so the Sedburghs would be able to see her. Then, after an absence of three and a half years, she had gone home to Scotland, taking her daughter with her.

Chapter Twelve

Western wind, when will thou blow,
The small rain down can rain?
Christ, that my love were in my arms
And I in my bed again!

—ANONYMOUS

It was May 18, 1815, less than a month before the battle of Waterloo ended forever Napoleon Bonaparte's dream of European domination. Ian Macdonald, who had wanted to fight in the war against Napoleon, was standing at Fort Charles, the sentinel built by the English to guard Kingston Harbor, thousands of miles away from Europe. His eyes were on the high mountains of Jamaica which lie behind Kingston, but his thoughts were far from the peaceful, tropical scene before him. He was thinking about war. Not the relatively civilized war that had been fought in Europe between opposing armies, but the brutal, agonizing *guerra a muerte* that had destroyed Venezuela.

They had been beaten. The brutal general José Tomás Bovés had managed to rally the semisavage llaneros, wild, deadly horsemen of the plains, and had loosed them all over the country to massacre republicans. Ian remembered vividly the battle that had ended it all. At La Puerta there had been 500 republicans against 2,300 under Tomás Bovés. Half the republicans had been left dead on the field, and Bovés had speared or shot all his prisoners.

Ian had been wounded in the shoulder but had made it to Caracas with Bolívar. The nightmare evacuation of Caracas, when ten thousand men, women and children had chosen to undertake the punishing long retreat to the coast rather than wait for Bovés, was mercifully vague in his mind, as he himself had been burning with fever during most of it. It was not until they had reached Margarita Island that Ian had received proper medical attention. If he had not been so physically tough he would have died.

They had been beaten. By the end of 1814 the republicans held only Margarita Island. Bovés had purged all existing republicans on the mainland, cutting the throats of prisoners, women, and children as he took town after town. A few scattered guerrilla republican bands still remained, but they were well hidden in remote and inaccessible places.

Ian had recently joined Bolívar in Jamaica in order to talk to the Duke of Manchester, the British governor. Bolívar had still not given up hope of winning British assistance in the fight for South American independence. Ian was cynical about the possibility of British help and not convinced of the wisdom of even applying for it, but he could not refuse to lend the support of his company when it was so urgently requested by his commander. He had been in Jamaica for about ten days, most of which time had been spent in deep discussion about the future of South America.

The Duke of Manchester was an enlightened and intelligent man who had listened with undisguised interest to Bolívar's analyses of his homeland's dilemma: "Our peoples have been kept in a state of childhood for three hundred years," he had told the Duke grimly while Ian listened in silent sympathy. "They have been forbidden to cultivate European crops, to manufacture goods, have been forced to do nothing but grow coffee, sugar, indigo, cotton, to keep herds on the savannas, and to mine the earth for gold—for the masters of the country." He was right, of course, but Britain was not going to move to support him with either money or arms.

"We are still allied to Spain," Manchester had said to Ian privately one day as they talked in the library of the governor's house. "Officially we are supporting Ferdinand, who is anxious to win back his South American empire. I can do nothing."

"I know that," Ian had replied. "He does too, I think. It is only the people of South America who can free themselves; no outside government, however powerful, can do it for them. He is feeling a little discouraged at the moment, that is all. He will recover."

The Duke had looked with curiosity at this tall dark Scotsman, Bolívar's trusted lieutenant. He could understand why the Venezuelan had been so anxious to have him come and why he had been so much more vigorous and hopeful since Macdonald's arrival. It was an intensely arresting face the Duke was regarding so attentively, deeply tanned, the mouth firm, the cheekbones high, the dark eyes full of laughter and of violence.

There was a total and unconscious arrogance about the man that made one instinctively look to him for leadership and for strength. He was so obviously unafraid for himself, had such an easy air of command about him, that his very presence was both invigorating and reassuring. "He will recover," the Duke repeated. "Doesn't that man know when he's beaten?"

Ian grinned, suddenly looking much younger. "Oh yes," he had replied, "he knows. He has been beaten twice now. But he is always ready to try again."

"And you, Mr. Macdonald," the Duke had asked, "will you accompany him once more?"

"I suppose so," Ian had answered somewhat offhandedly.

The Duke had stared at him with frank curiosity. "Don't you miss home?" he questioned.

Ian's vivid, mobile face had become suddenly still. "Sometimes," he said evenly, and changed the subject.

He was thinking of that conversation now as he stood above the turquoise splendor of Kingston Harbor watching the mountains so clearly silhouetted against the blue sky. "Don't you miss home?" the Duke had asked, and now he saw before him not the tropical mountains of Jamaica but the misty, towering mountains of Lochaber, shrouded in cloud and silvered by rain. A sudden, savage pain clawed at his heart. But it was not of the mountains that he was thinking, or even Scotland itself. "Frances," he said softly, and his face took on a withdrawn and brooding look, an aspect so bleak and forbidding that the native who was approaching him abruptly stopped and turned away.

He had tried not to think of her. Ever since the news of her marriage had come from Douglas he had resolutely tried to put her from his thoughts. But always, at the back of his mind, there was an aching sense of emptiness and loss. He was like a man without a center; the one thing in his life that had been necessary to his happiness was gone. He could live without her, but he felt as though he were in perpetual exile, a stranger in a land that was bleak and empty and devoid of meaning. Fruitlessly he had tried to tell himself that she wasn't worth this pain, that she did not love him, that she had refused to marry him and then married someone else as soon as he was out of sight. He had not been successful in subduing the haunting sense of loss. Now he turned slowly and rode through the narrow streets of Port Royal back to King's House where he was engaged to have dinner. He was met by the Duke's secretary. "Oh, Mr. Macdonald, the ship from Margarita Island was carrying a letter for you from England. Captain Nevans left it with His Grace just a few hours ago."

Ian put out an imperative hand. He had not heard from home for over two years now. He had written finally from Margarita Island after he was recovered enough to know he was going to be all right. He looked now at the paper in his hand. It was from Douglas. He smiled briefly at Mr. Bellington. "Thank you." He took the letter out into the garden, sat down by himself on a stone bench, opened it and began to read:

Dear Ian,

You must come home at once. I have bad news for you. Charlie is dead. He was shot by a crofter—one of the crofters evicted in the Strathnaver Clearance in Sutherland. The bullet was evidently meant for Lord

Stafford, the Countess of Sutherland's husband. He and Charlie were riding together when it happened. The crofter has been apprehended and will be tried, but Charlie is dead.

You must come home. You are Lochaber now and you are sorely needed. Your mother and sister are too distressed to write, but asked me to convey their love and their desire to see you soon.

I was most relieved to receive your letter from Margarita Island. The news from Venezuela has been disastrous and we have all been profoundly worried about you. Thank God you are safe.

One other thing I feel I must mention. From your letter it was apparent that you had not received my own earlier letters to you. There is some news you should know. Robert Sedburgh, Frances's husband, has been dead for almost two years now. She is living in Edinburgh with her father. She, too, has been very worried about your safety.

Ian, you must come home. We all need you now. Hoping your next communication will be in person I remain,

Your Cousin, Douglas Macdonald.

Ian read the letter through twice, then sat staring at it sightlessly for some ten more minutes. Finally he rose and went into the house. He spent the night in deep conversation with Colonel Bolívar and boarded a British ship the next morning. After five long years of war, Ian Macdonald was going home.

For Frances the two years since Robert's death had moved slowly. She had gone to London as she had promised her father- and mother-in-law, and after her official period of mourning was over the marriage proposals had rained in once more. Charlie Macdonald had been one of her suitors this time. It had led to some stress between Frances and Lady Lochaber, who had been extremely anxious to see Charlie married. Frances wouldn't marry him and he refused to marry anyone else, and the result was that Lady Lochaber had no grandchildren and Lochaber had no heir except Ian, who was also unmarried. Lady Lochaber tended to blame Frances for that too.

She had learned to hide her feelings. The news from Venezuela had been agonizing. She had had to rely on Douglas, who had cultivated a friendship with Andrés Bello, the Venezuelan Representative in London. First they learned of the disastrous battle of La Puerta and then of the retreat from Caracas. It was six months before Ian's letter from Margarita Island had reached Douglas.

He was beautifully tactful. He had merely sent her the letter, without comment. He had not come himself, so no one was there to see her face when she had opened it.

He was safe. For many minutes that was all she could register, the tears coursing silently down her cheeks. Then, firmly disciplining her emotions, she had read the letter through. "There is scarcely a province left," Ian had written. "Towns which had thousands of inhabitants are now reduced to a few hundred or even a few dozen. Of others, there are nothing but vestiges, to show that they were once inhabited by human beings. Roads and fields are full of unburied corpses; whole villages have been burnt, whole families are nothing but a memory. Those republicans who are still alive are poor as Christ, stricken with fever, with one foot in prison and the other in exile. That, Douglas, is what war means in Venezuela.

"Considering the above, it is strange to have to say that although this war, in which I played so ineffectual a part, has left me with memories that are mostly evil, I do not wish that I had missed it. When you have had a glimpse of such a disaster as this, the result is not necessarily disillusionment and cynicism. I do not exactly know why, but it is so." She read the rest of the letter with mixed feelings. He had written to his mother, he said. He asked Douglas to write to him. He did not mention the possibility of coming home. He did not mention her.

She had folded the letter on her lap and stared sightlessly out the window, allowing her thoughts for once to find their homing. Ian. Ever since Robert had died she had waited for him. All through the years of her marriage she had rigorously suppressed her feelings for him, but her love had always been there, a swift and perilous current beneath the surface of her life. She closed her eyes and the memory that could no longer summon up Rob brought her Ian's face. When she had met him her life had been diverted into new channels, rushing wildly over rocks and rapids, far from the still, quiet pools of her childhood. She had wanted the serenity she had lost and she had wanted Ian as well. To get them she had wagered her happiness, her honor, and the honor of her family. She had lost. She opened her eyes and looked now at the letter that held no mention of her.

"Oh my love," she whispered. "I could do without peace, even, if only I were with you."

Three weeks later Charles Macdonald, fourth Earl of Lochaber, was shot to death by a Sutherland crofter.

Chapter Thirteen

O where ha you been, Lord Randal, my son?
And where ha you been, my handsome young man?
—ANONYMOUS

Ian's ship put down anchor at Spithead and he made the
rest of the journey to Scotland by land. He went up the
west coast, through Carlisle and Glasgow, along Loch
Lomond and into the Highlands. As he rode through the
towering, awesome beauty of Glen Orchy Ian found
himself staring at the mountains of his native land like a
starved lover who after many years of absence is finally
reunited with the object of his dreams. He could not
look enough at the high, green slopes, at the carpets of
fern and of heather, at the rushing little burns and the
still clearnesses of the lochs. By the time he reached the
hauntingly beautiful desolation of Glencoe he was horrified to discover the sting of tears behind his eyes. Never
had he felt more profoundly the ancient ties that bound
him to this land. Never had he loved Scotland more
then now when he was home after five years of volun-
tary exile. As he saw the towers of Castle Hunter

through eyes that were unaccountably blurry, he swore to himself that he would never leave her again.

His mother was in the garden when he arrived at Castle Hunter and saw his horse crossing the causeway. She ran into the house and met him in the front hall. Ian held her to him tightly, listening to her repeat his name over and over. It was five months since Charlie's death. Finally she stepped back, brushing at her cheeks with her fingers. "What a welcome!" she said, with an effort at lightness. "Come upstairs to the drawing room, Ian."

But when they reached the white-paneled room filled with comfortable, chintz-covered furniture, Ian had been shocked by his mother's appearance. She had aged twenty years. No wonder, he thought grimly. Of the three sons she had borne and reared he was the only one still living. He thought of his sister, the family baby who had been twelve when he left. "Where is Margaret?" he asked.

"She went into Kinlochlevin," Lady Lochaber replied. "She has been such a comfort to me, Ian! I don't know what I would have done without her."

"I am so sorry, Mama," he said soberly. "I came as soon as I could."

Her head, once so dark but now heavily silvered, bowed. "He never knew what happened, Ian. He died instantly. At least he didn't suffer. I suppose that's some comfort."

He went over to where she was seated on the sofa, sat down beside her, and put an arm around her shoulders. "How can I help?" he asked gently.

Her spine stiffened and she blew her nose. "You can

stay home, for one thing," she said with a touch of her usual asperity.

"I will," he said soberly. His eyes went around the familiar, well-loved room. "I promise."

Her brown eyes looked into his. "There is trouble in Scotland, Ian. That crofter who shot Charlie is just an example of what is happening here. His wife had been burned to death in the Strathnaver Clearance."

He looked incredulous. "Burned?"

"Yes. The factor had given the crofters six months' notice to leave. Well of course they didn't move. Where were they to go, for heaven's sake? Anyway, after six months the factor—Sellar was his name—moved into the valley with men, dogs, and fire. They burned down the houses. The old wife of this man didn't have time to get out."

"Dhé!" said Ian softly. "So it has come to this."

"Yes. It is happening all over the Highlands."

"Not here!" said Ian quickly.

"No, not here. But I will tell you that Charlie talked about it. The land is overpopulated and the rents that come in do not go far when you are living mostly in London." Lady Lochaber's voice was carefully neutral.

Ian shot her a look and then picked up her hand. "There will be no clearances in Lochaber, Mama. I promise you that, too."

Lady Lochaber blinked and patted his hand. "You have the chieftain's love of his land, Ian. You get that from your father."

"I'm almost glad Dada isn't around to see what is going on today," Ian said grimly. "It would break his heart."

"I know." Her eyes narrowed a little. "I'll tell you

something else that would break his heart, my son."

"What is that, Mama?"

"Lochaber passing into the hands of strangers because his own sons refused to marry and produce an heir!"

Ian looked at her cautiously. "Oh," he said.

"Yes, 'oh'!" she replied tartly. "Not one grandchild do I have. It is your duty, Ian, to marry. God knows I tried to impress that fact on your brother, with what result you can see."

"Why didn't Charlie marry?" Ian asked curiously.

Lady Lochaber compressed her lips. "Why?" she said, with awful calm. "For the same reason, Ian, that at least eight other men of my personal acquaintance have not married. Not to mention another odd dozen or so strewn around London."

"Oh," Ian said again. "Frances."

"Yes, Frances. Really, Ian, I am quite annoyed with her. If she plans to spend the rest of her life mourning Robert Sedburgh she ought to have the decency to stay away from eligible men. Every time I thought Charlie was on the verge of offering for some girl he would run into Frances and it would start all over again."

"I see. Well, Mama," he said soothingly, "if anything happens to me Lochaber won't go to a stranger. Douglas is next in line after me, you know."

"And is Douglas married?" Lady Lochaber asked inexorably.

"Well, no, but . . ."

"But me no buts," his mother snapped. "Douglas won't get married for the same reason as Charlie."

Ian looked slightly amused. "Don't you think you're being rather hard on Frances, Mama?"

"No." She looked at him shrewdly. "I always thought you and Frances would make a match of it."

"We found we didn't agree," he responded shortly.

"I see." After a moment she smiled at him and tactfully changed the subject. "I'm glad you're home, Ian. We've all missed you."

"I'm glad to be home, Mama," he responded. "I missed you too."

A few hours later Ian was in the library, reacquainting himself, when the door opened and his sister came in. "Hello, Ian!" she said, coming to kiss him. "It's good to see you."

He returned her kiss then stepped back to look at her, surprise clearly written on his face. "Margaret," he said slowly. "I hardly recognized you." The girl he was looking at was tall and slim, with clear olive skin, dark eyes, and shining black hair worn smoothly coiled on top of her head. She was lovely. He grinned at her. "I remember you as a brat with pigtails and dirty fingernails."

She smiled back. "I'm seventeen now. You've been gone a long time, Ian."

He shook his head. "I suppose I have." He gestured to the two wing chairs positioned before the fireplace. "Sit down, Maggie, and tell me what's been going on around here."

She sighed and obeyed him. "Nothing very happy, I'm afraid, Ian," she replied. "Have you heard about the clearances?"

"Mama told me something about them. There were some clearances before I left but I gather it has gotten worse."

"Much worse. Cattle prices have fallen since the war has ended and the fishing has become less profitable as well. More and more landlords are clearing their land of crofters in order to put in sheep. One can't argue with them on the bases of economics. Sheep are definitely more profitable. But they are destroying us as a nation. From time immemorial the Highlands have been a collective culture. We have stood together against the Lowlands and against the English. Now, with one blow, the chiefs are destroying their own civilization." Margaret's young face looked somber. "It is ugly, Ian. What happened to Charlie is a measure of that."

"But there have been no clearances in Lochaber."

"No. And, my dear brother, I'll tell you who you have to thank for that."

"Mama?"

"No. She was against them, of course, but Charlie wouldn't let himself be swayed by Mama."

Ian frowned. "Then who?"

"Frances."

Ian's black brows shot up. "Frances!"

"Yes." A look of satisfaction came over Margaret's face. "I shall always feel privileged that I heard the dressing down she gave to Charlie when he mentioned to her the possibility of putting in sheep. She told him he was a disgrace to his name, to his family, and to his nation. She said he was worse than a Campbell. She said that in her opinion the highest title a man could hold was that of a Scottish chief, that the Sassenach title of earl meant nothing compared to that. She told him that Dada would turn in his grave if ever a man of his blood evicted his people from the land. 'I mind always some words Ian told me your father once said,' she told

Charlie. 'They have always seemed to me to exemplify the code of a true chieftain. He said that he thanked God that he had never betrayed his trust, never injured the poor, and never refused a share of what he had to the stranger and the needy.' Then she ended up with the coup de grâce.''

"And what was that?" Ian asked in a carefully expressionless voice.

"She told him she'd never speak to him again if even one crofter was removed from Macdonald land. That ended any more talk from Charlie about clearing Lochaber. He wanted desperately to marry Frances."

"So I hear," Ian said in the same expressionless tone. "From what Mama tells me, his desire was not singular."

Margaret looked at him in awe. "Ian, I don't think even Mary Queen of Scots had as many suitors as Frances. I stayed with her at Charlotte Square for a month last spring. Really, I don't see why she is wasting herself in a backwater like Edinburgh. She could hold almost any position she wanted to. Why, the Duke of Pendleton drove up from London just to see her! He has royal blood, you know. His mother was a princess."

There was a faint, sardonic smile on Ian's face. "Frances has royal blood, too," he said. "She is a Stewart. Her ancestors were kings in Scotland while the Hanovers were still mucking out pigstyes."

"Ian!" Margaret's eyes were alight with laughter. "That is just what Frances said."

He grinned. "Good for her. Frances may be the most obstinate woman on the face of the earth but, on most matters, she has got her priorities in order."

Margaret suddenly sobered. "Yes, she does. At present her chief priority is Nell, but she's got to stop living in the past some time. She never talks about her husband, but I'm afraid she thinks about him. Why else would she have so little interest in the men who surround her?''

Ian didn't answer. He found he could not bear to talk about Robert Sedburgh or his daughter. The sudden, savage jealousy his sister's mention of them had provoked in his breast was a grim reminder that more than just an ocean had divided him from Frances these past five years.

Chapter Fourteen

O where have you been, my long long love,
These long seven years and mair?

—ANONYMOUS

Ian stayed six days at Castle Hunter and then he left for Edinburgh. He told his mother and sister he was going to see his solicitor; in reality he was going to see Frances.

Edinburgh. Frances lived in Charlotte Square, one of the glories of the New Town built in the late eighteenth century after the North Loch had been drained and bridged by an enlightened town council. As Ian rode down Princes Street his eyes went with affection and respect to the towering heights of Edinburgh Castle, for so many centuries the home and fortress of Scotland's kings. The classical New Town was Edinburgh's pride, but Ian loved the Old Town, with its high, narrow houses, winding closes, and boisterous, teeming life. The Macdonalds in fact still had a house on the Canongate, a short distance from the Palace of Holyroodhouse.

He asked for Lady Robert in a constricted voice and

gave his name. The servant went to inform Frances and then came back to conduct him to the drawing room. She was standing by the tall windows, which were opened to let in the warm August air. The sunlight reflected off her pale hair and bathed her face in the merciless light that was kind to very few women. Her hands were tightly clasped together in front of her, her eyes were deeply green, unsmiling and intent as they rested on him, standing bareheaded and enormous in her doorway.

He gave a strange laugh. "I don't know how it is, Frances, but you always turn out to be more beautiful in the flesh than one remembered you."

She, who had received unmoved the lavish compliments of England's greatest and wealthiest nobles, flushed. "And somehow you are always bigger than one remembered," she returned with an attempt at lightness. As he crossed the room toward her she said a trifle breathlessly, "I am so sorry about Charlie. It must have been quite a shock to you."

He stood directly before her now. "It was," he replied grimly. "It was also a shock to learn that you were a widow. I had not received any of Douglas's previous letters."

"Oh," she said faintly and looked up into his lean, tanned face. The brilliant life was still there in his eyes, but it was controlled now. He looked different, she thought confusedly. He was not really any taller than she remembered, it was the sense of authority he exuded that was new. He had not said he was sorry about Robert's death. Her chin rose a trifle. "Has Margaret told you what is going on in the Highlands?"

"Yes. And I gather I have you to thank for saving Lochaber from Charlie's greed."

Her finely arched brows drew together. "Nonsense. Your mother would never have allowed him to carry out any clearances. I merely reinforced what I'm sure he had heard before." Her lips set. "I'm sorry Charlie was killed, but I am not sorry you are Lochaber now. The Highlands need chiefs like you. Too many of them have been seduced by the lure of Sassenach money."

He was not surprised by her reaction. Abstract causes would never have any appeal for Frances, but she had always been endlessly concerned about the people she knew. "What chiefs are refusing to be seduced?" he asked her, a faint approving smile in his eyes.

She grimaced slightly. "I hate to say it, but the Duke of Argyll is one of the more notable holdouts. Of course, he already has so much money he can scarecely need more."

He looked thoughtful. The Duke of Argyll, Mac Caileinmhor, was chief of the Clan Campbell the hereditary enemy of the Stewarts and the Macdonalds. Centuries of hatred and oceans of blood lay between the Campbells and the other clans of the central Highlands and none had more cause to hate them than the Macdonalds of Glencoe.

There was a knock at the door and it opened softly. A small dark gold head peeked into the room. "I'm home, Mama," said Nell.

"Come in, darling," Frances responded, walking past Ian to take her daughter's hand. "There is someone here I want you to meet This is Ian Macdonald, Douglas's cousin who has been in South America. He is the Earl of Lochaber now." She braced herself slightly as

Nell looked gravely at Ian. This was a meeting she had had nightmares about.

Ian's face looked strained and harsh as he unwillingly regarded Frances's daughter. She was all Stewart, he was relieved to see. There was nothing of Robert Sedburgh in the dark gray eyes or small square chin. He raised his brows slightly and looked at Frances. She said in a calm, self-possessed voice, "You don't have to say it. She's the image of my father, I know. She looks more like him every year. It's positively uncanny."

Nell took two steps toward Ian. "Are you a pirate?" she inquired in her clear child's voice.

Ian suddenly grinned. "No. Do I look like a pirate to you?"

Nell smiled back. "Yes. You look just like the pirate in a book my Poppy gave me. But you need a patch over your eye."

"Where *is* Poppy?" Frances put in before Ian could answer. "I thought he took you to Arthur's Seat with him."

"He did, Mama. And we climbed *half way* up." Her gray eyes sparkled. "I'll bet Stephanie Scott never climbed up that far, and she's four and a half already."

"You are getting to be a first-rate mountaineer, darling, but where is your grandfather?"

"He went to the university, Mama. He told me to tell you."

"Thank you. Now you may go upstairs. Nurse is waiting for you."

"All right." The little girl went slowly toward the door then turned to smile again at Ian. "Did you kill a lot of soldiers in South America?" she asked irrepressibly.

"I'm afraid I did," he answered gravely.

"How many?"

"Hundreds, I believe." His dark eyes were steady on her face.

"Hundreds! Wait until I tell Stephanie Scott!"

"Nell," said Frances purposefully, and the little girl grinned impishly.

"I'm going, Mama. Goodbye . . ." She frowned in sudden confusion. "How can he be Lord Lochaber?" she asked Frances. "Lord Lochaber is someone else."

"Don't you remember I told you Lord Lochaber was shot by a bad man?" Frances asked steadily.

"Oh." Nell looked gravely at Ian.

"Not by Ian!" Frances said hastily and Nell looked indignant.

"I know that!" she said. "He shooted the people in South America!" With another smile at Ian she finally departed, closing the door behind her.

Frances turned to Ian a rueful smile in her eyes. "Nell is regrettably bloodthirsty," she said.

"So I see." Amusement colored his voice. "Who, may I ask, is Stephanie Scott?"

"Nell's greatest friend and rival. She lives across the square."

"And she's four and a half already," he said with mock gravity.

"Yes," said Frances, conscious of treading on dangerous ground. She opened her mouth to change the subject but Ian was already speaking.

"Nell is quite tall, isn't she?" He frowned. "How old is she, anyway? Three?"

"No, she is just four," she responded cautiously. Her long green eyes were veiled as they looked at him and, returning her look, he felt suddenly a wave of desire so strong that it startled him and, to conceal his feeling, he said hastily, "When was she born?"

Frances kept looking at him. "May eighteenth," she responded.

There was a moment's silence then Ian's eyes focused in a way that set her heart racing. "*May* eighteenth?" he said sharply.

"She came early," Frances said quietly. "She wasn't due until July but I had a fall. It was quite nasty, actually. I knocked myself out. She came that night." She was conscious that she was talking too much and stopped abruptly.

Ian's black brows were drawn together and there was a little flame burning deep within his eyes. "May," he said. "Exactly nine months after you and I . . ." He broke off, a look of astonishment on his face. "Sweet Jesus, Frances, she's mine, isn't she?"

Her face was shuttered. "Would you believe me if I said she wasn't?"

His dark eyes held hers relentlessly. Under that look her own gaze fell. "No," he said grimly. "I wouldn't believe you." He looked at her slightly bent head. "Why?" he asked. He sounded very angry. "Why did you lie to me? I was afraid of that. I asked you."

"I know." Her voice was muffled.

"*Why*, Frances?"

She raised her head, stared back at him and told him the truth. "Because it was between you and me, that's why. No one else. Just the two of us." Her mouth quivered. "Besides, I never thought you would really go."

He prowled to the door and back, his long stride making the room seem much smaller than it was. He

116

finally paused beside her. "It never occurred to you to write and tell me?" he said evenly. "I would have come home."

"You were thousands of miles away," she said bitterly. "How long would it have been before you even got my letter let alone returned? Time, after all, was a factor, Ian."

His face was bleak. "So you told Sedburgh," he said.

"Yes." The bitterness had left her voice. Ian would never make the mistake of thinking she would do anything else. "I was frightened. You were gone. I didn't know what to do and he was so kind. So I told him and he offered to marry me."

"What a hero." His tone was sardonic.

"Yes, he was," she replied forcefully. "I prayed, Ian. Mother Mary, how I prayed that she would be a girl. Rob would have accepted a boy as his, would have made him heir to all of Aysgarth. He would have done that for me. Yes, I think he was a hero."

"I see." He wondered if she would ever understand what this knowledge meant to him. He had left her to bear his child in another man's house, to be reared with another man's name. His woman. His child. Given away to another man. He stared down at the face that had haunted his dreams for five long years. There was a strained look about her eyes but nothing could mar the miraculously clear lines of the bones. She sounded as if she had loved Sedburgh. He felt savage. And so he said the words he had come halfway across the world to say, but the phrasing was not what he had intended. "I hope you won't refuse to marry me now?" he asked.

Frances was watching him with a face as shuttered

and remote as a Byzantine madonna. "Why? So that you can have Nell?"

"I want Nell," he answered. "And I want you." For a long moment they looked at each other, steadily and with something that was almost hostility. His eyes were dark and brilliant, fierce, not loving. He pulled her into his arms and, unresisting, she went. His kiss was hard with the pent-up passion of many years. She closed her eyes, melting effortlessly into his embrace, helpless as ever against her love for him. His anger was drowned in desire.

When he finally raised his head to look down at her his eyes were black. "Will you marry me?" he said, but this time he spoke in Gaelic.

Her mouth curved in a beautiful smile. "Of course I'll marry you," she replied in the same language.

He grinned, his dark face lighting with that blazing life she saw every day in her daughter's smile. "When?"

"Whenever you like."

"Next week, then. I'll get a special license."

"All right," she said with a semblance of her old serenity. "It might be a little hard on Nell. You'll have to have patience with her. But she'll get used to it."

"We'll have her name changed to Macdonald." he said purposefully.

He saw her stiffen. "No," she said quickly.

He frowned. "What do you mean 'no'? I am her father. She should have my name."

"Oh, Ian," she said helplessly, "can't you understand? She is yours by birth and she will be yours by upbringing, too, but for the first two years of her life she was Rob's. He gave her the protection of his name at a time when she desperately needed it. And he loved

118

her so. I can't do that to him, Ian. It would be like saying he never existed.''

''But she is a Macdonald!'' Centuries of tribal pride sounded in those words.

''Nevertheless, her name will remain Sedburgh.'' There was an expression on his face that she did not like at all. ''Besides,'' she added, ''if we change her name people may suspect the truth and that would not do at all.'' She was sorry she had not thought of that reason first.

''If no one has guessed by now they are hardly likely to at this late date,'' he said impatiently.

''Who said no one had guessed?''

He gave her a long straight look. ''Who?'' he asked abruptly.

''Douglas.''

''Oh, Douglas.'' There was a pause. ''How did he know?''

''You may not have noticed, my love,'' she said softly, ''but when Nell smiles she is the image of you. It is a similarity that is not going to go unrecognized. I think we can pass it off as imitation, since it is a similarity of expression and not of features. But I wouldn't want to give any more food to the gossip mongers.''

''I suppose so,'' he said unwillingly.

There was the sound of a door closing and voices in the hall. Then the door to the drawing room opened and Sir Donal Stewart came in. ''Ian! Thank God you've come home. We have all been so worried about you.'' There was a slight tinge of reproof in Sir Donal's gentle tone. He had never totally approved of Ian. Robert Sedburgh had been much more to his taste. However, he smiled kindly and asked about the Macdonald family. Nor did he show any sign of disappointment when

Frances told him about the upcoming marriage. He had long since resigned himself to the inevitable. Though he had never said anything to Frances, Sir Donal had not missed Nell's occasional resemblance to Ian. "Well, that news should cheer your mother up immeasurably," he said merely. "She has been longing to have a son married for years."

"Don't I know it," groaned Frances. "Really, Ian, I feel like Helen of Troy meeting Hecuba every time I have to face her. It wasn't my fault Charlie wanted to marry me. I certainly didn't encourage him."

Ian shouted with laughter. "Well, all will be forgiven now, I'm sure, once I tell her I'm going to do my duty by the family and marry you."

Her green eyes mocked him. "Your nobility overwhelms me, my lord."

"It does me too," he replied cheerfully. Then he looked at her more carefully. "Seriously, Frances, do you think you could live with my mother? I don't think I can ask her to leave Castle Hunter . . ."

"Good God!" She sounded appalled. "Of course you can't ask her to leave. It is her home. We will get along fine. We always did, until this business of Charlie came up."

Twin devils danced in his eyes. "And Douglas too," he said.

She looked startled. "Douglas? Surely she doesn't think Douglas wants to marry me?"

"Douglas and at least eight other men of her personal acquaintance. Not to mention the dozens more that are scattered around London."

"She didn't say that."

"She did. What is more my sister informed me that

120

she didn't think even Mary Queen of Scots had as many suitors as you."

She gave him an austere look. "Then you can count yourself fortunate, my lord, to have won such a prize."

"You always did like pirates," he replied smoothly. "It must run in the family."

Chapter Fifteen

As fair art thou, my bonnie lass,
   So deep in luve am I;
And I will luve thee still, my dear,
   Till a' the seas gang dry.

               —ROBERT BURNS

There was universal rejoicing among the mothers of Edinburgh and London when Frances Sedburgh married Ian Macdonald, fifth Earl of Lochaber. The ceremony took place in the small chapel at Castle Hunter, there being a marked shortage of Catholic churches in Edinburgh. The happiest mother of all—the Dowager Countess of Lochaber—was in attendance.

Lady Lochaber had embraced Ian with enthusiasm when he had told her the good news. "I am so happy, Ian! You know how I have always loved Frances."

There was amusement in his eyes, but he held his peace. "Frances voiced the same sentiments about you, Mama," he said merely.

Lady Lochaber shot him a look. "I know what you're thinking, so get that smug expression off your face."

123

He laughed. "She did, though. She also said that she would enjoy very much sharing a house with you. You know Frances, Mama. She meant it."

His mother smiled a little mistily. "I know. Frances has always had a disposition as lovely as her face. She has never said an unpleasant word to me and I must admit I was not overly sympathetic about her rejection of Charlie."

Ian grinned. "Frances saves all her bad temper for me. That is why she is such an angel to everyone else."

"You would put the virgin herself into a temper," Lady Lochaber said tartly. "I hope you mean to settle down and mend your ways."

He assumed such a pious expression that his sister, who had just come into the room, giggled. "I am a reformed man, Mother." he said gravely.

"Hmn," his mother replied. "We shall see."

Frances and Ian spent the two weeks of their honeymoon at the Macdonalds' lodge on Loch Shiel. The late summer weather was warm and clear and they spent a great deal of time sailing and fishing, both activities that Ian loved and had sorely missed. His tropical tan returned and even Frances's skin turned a pale golden hue. They were having lunch out of a picnic basket one afternoon a few days before they were due to leave when the subject of the clearances came up. Ian had stretched himself out on the ground while Frances packed up the remains of the lunch. He propped his chin on his hands and watched her for a moment in silence. She had her hair tied up on top of her head in a topknot secured by a green ribbon that matched her eyes. Her cheeks were the color of peaches from the sun. "I think I am going to pay a visit to the Duke of Argyll," he said slowly.

She dropped the napkin she was holding. "Argyll!" she said in a startled tone. "Why, Ian?"

"Because I will need help if I am going to save Lochaber." His voice was grim.

There was a long silence. "Charlie spent a lot of money," she said finally.

"He did."

"Your mother won't like it," she said positively. "No one will like it, Ian. Mac Caileinmhor!"

He gave a twisted smile. "You might as well be saying 'Satan' from your tone."

"I might as well," she agreed. "That is how the Campbells are regarded in Lochaber."

He rolled over on his back, put his hands behind his head, and narrowed his eyes against the sky. "I learned one thing in Venezuela, Frances," he said in a quiet voice. "And that is if a nation cannot unite to fight a common enemy it is doomed. The Highlands are besieged. Argyll is one of the great Highland leaders and you tell me he is resisting the land clearances. I want to resist the land clearances. It makes sense that we work together. The past is over with; it is the present that matters now. And the future." He paused then said neutrally, "Can you understand that, Frances?"

"Yes," she replied slowly. "Yes, I can. But what about the rest of the clan? What will they think? It might be the best thing for the Highlands, as you say, but it won't necessarily be the best thing for you, Ian."

He looked amused. "Jesus, sweetheart, when have you ever known me to do the thing that was best for me?" His eyes closed. "But I wanted you to understand," he said sleepily. "The rest of them will come around eventually."

He went to sleep and she finished packing the basket, then sat beside him looking down at his quiet face. He had been restless last night, waking her with his tossing. He had been muttering something in Spanish that she had not been able to understand. But he was sleeping peacefully now and she sat thankfully, listening to the gentle lapping of the loch against the shore, her eyes on his unguarded, tranquil face. They were leaving Loch Shiel for Lochaber in two days' time and Frances realized suddenly that she did not want to go. Even Nell seemed so far removed from her now. She was too filled with Ian.

For five years she had submerged her feelings for him and now they raged like a mountain burn in springtime. She reached out and gently touched the shock of think black hair that had fallen over his forehead. She loved him. More—she adored him. She always had. She always would. She was pleased that he wanted her to understand about his approaching the Campbells, but he needn't have worried. She would have agreed to anything he proposed. The only time she had ever held out against him was over the matter of his joining the army. She had been wrong, she thought now, sitting on the quiet shore of Loch Shiel. Douglas had been right when he told her that she was trying to smash the very qualities in Ian that she loved. Robert Sedburgh had been the kind of husband she had wanted Ian to be. She had come to care for Rob, but she had not grown dizzy and wild whenever he came near her. He was not like Ian. No one was like Ian.

His lashes lifted and she found herself looking into

the dark depths of his eyes. "Did you have a nice sleep?" she asked.

"Mnn." He held out a hand to her. "Lie down with me."

She read correctly the look in his eyes and glanced around her nervously. "There's no one here," he said in his deep, slow voice.

"What if someone should come by," she protested, but she let him draw her down beside him. The grass was warm under her back. She felt his hands on the buttons of her dress, then his lips found her warm flesh. She quivered and he looked up. Her eyes were green as the grass she was lying on. Through the haze of passion she heard his voice. "You are so sweet, Frances. So sweet . . ."

The day they were to leave to return to Castle Hunter Ian woke early. They had not drawn the curtains last night, and the sun poured in the window, spilling over Frances's ash gold hair on the pillow beside him. He turned and regarded her slender back. He kissed her ear and she burrowed deeper into the pillow. "Wake up," he said inexorably. "We have to make an early start."

She made noises of protest then, when his hand pulled the warm cover off her shoulder, she yelped in indignation. "Wake up," he said again.

Reluctantly she rolled over and stared at him reproachfully. "I wouldn't be so tired in the morning if you'd let me sleep at night."

Ian laughed softly, low in his throat, stretched himself and yawned. "You never complain at night," he said.

She cast her eyes down meekly. "That's because I'm a dutiful wife."

His dark eyes were full of laughter. "I can think of many adjectives to describe you, mo chridhe," he said, "and none of them is 'dutiful.' "

"What adjectives would you use?" she asked sweetly.

"Stubborn," he replied. "Obstinate, self-willed, immovable . . ."

"Stop!" Her eyes rested on him inscrutably. "You're not very flattering."

He stretched and yawned again, shoulder muscles bunching lazily with the slow movement of his arms. "I never flatter you," he said.

"No. You don't."

He turned at the tone of her voice. There was a warm half-sleepy remoteness in her beauty that caused him to lean toward her. Her eyes glinted. "I thought you were in a hurry."

"I am." He bent and kissed her with a casual possessiveness that deepened in intensity as she responded. He raised his head and a very faint smile lifted her lips as she gazed limpidly back.

He looked amused. "You are a devil," he said softly.

Her eyes widened. "Well, are we making an early start?" she asked innocently.

"Castle Hunter can wait," he murmured. "I just thought of something I have to do first."

Ian's mother and sister were not as amenable as Frances to his decision to seek help from the Duke of Argyll. "You cannot mean it!" Margaret exclaimed when he mentioned at dinner he was going to Inverary.

"I do," he replied imperturbably as he cut his meat.

His mother put down her wine glass and stared at him with compressed lips. "Have you forgotten what the Campbells have done to this nation, to this family? You have been away for too long, my son, if you talk of making common cause with Mac Caileinmhor. It was the Campbells who rose up and massacred our innocent people in 1692. It was the Campbells who fought with the German king against Prince Charles in 1745. It was the Campbells who grew rich as the loyal chiefs were stripped of their lands and their power after Culloden. They are the enemy, Ian. I would rather starve than take a bite of food from the hands of a Campbell."

Ian had listened to his mother attentively and now he put down his fork and looked at her for a moment in silence. She was dressed in a fashionable evening gown. Her hair was arranged simply but in excellent taste. She looked like the essence of civilization as she sat at the polished table in the beautifully paneled room. But she was a Highlander, Cameron by birth and Macdonald by marriage. She had tribal loyalties never dreamed of by the polished sophisticates of the south. Well, he had them too. It was not going to be easy to go, hat in hand, to his hereditary enemy. But what he had seen in Venezuela had made a profound impression on Ian Macdonald. "I need money, mother," he said finally. "I have an idea that might help put Lochaber back on its feet again, economically. But to put it into practice will require more money than I can lay my hands on."

"You are going to ask Mac Caileinmhor if you can borrow money from him?" Margaret sounded incredulous.

"I want to borrow money from a bank," he replied patiently. "But I am an unknown factor. If the Duke of

Argyll gives me a reference I will have a much better chance of getting the money I need.''

''The last time the Macdonalds went to Inverary it was in the army of the great Marquis of Montrose. *Your* great-great-grandfather,'' Lady Lochaber said as she turned to Frances. ''They went to bring fire and sword to the Campbells in their own land and they chased Mac Caileinmhor out of his own castle.'' She paused. ''What do you think of this, Frances?''

Frances's face maintained its expression of unruffled serenity. ''I think Ian is right, Godmama. The Campbells have used us for long enough. Now it is time for us to use them.''

Lady Lochaber looked thoughtful and Ian shot his wife a glance of amused respect. Trust Frances to find the right way of putting it. Wisely he said no more, and after a minute Lady Lochaber changed the subject. He left a week later for Inverary.

Chapter Sixteen

Argyll has raised a hunder men,
  An hunder harness'd rarely,
And he's awa' by the back of Dunkell
  To plunder the castle of Airlie.

— ANONYMOUS

The week before he left for Campbell country, Ian devoted to trying to win over Nell. It was uphill work but he persevered with a patience that Frances had not known he possessed.

Nell was not happy about her mother's marriage. Frances had known it would be a difficult time for her but she hadn't realized the extent to which Nell would be upset. It had begun as soon as Frances broke the news to her. "My Papa is dead," Nell had said stubbornly. "I don't want another Papa." And nothing Frances could say would soften her.

The news that they would be leaving Charlotte Square to go live at Castle Hunter, was, if anything, even more traumatic. Nell began to cling to Frances in the way she had after Robert Sedburgh's death. She didn't want to leave the house. She followed her grandfather about like a determined shadow and she showed a face of implacable hostility to Ian.

"I don't want you to marry my mother!" she shouted at him the afternoon before he left for Lochaber. "You aren't my Papa!"

The bleak look that had settled over Ian's face pulled at Frances's heart. She had taken Nell upstairs and then returned to find him in front of the mantel staring down into the empty grate. He looked relaxed but his white knuckles on the mantelpiece gave him away. "You are going to have to be patient with Nell, Ian," she said, looking anxiously at his bent head. "She has had some very hard things to cope with for such a little girl. This isn't easy for her."

"So I see." His voice was level.

"She adored Rob, you see," she went on, conscious that she was inflicting hurt but aware of the necessity for it. "She was only two when he died but she was old enough to miss him and to grieve for him. We stayed at Aysgarth, which helped. Rob's parents love her and have always paid a lot of attention to her, which helped also. Then we came back home to Edinburgh and she was uprooted and upset again."

He had turned to look at her. "Why did you leave Aysgarth, Frances?"

She shrugged a little. "There was no place for me there with Rob gone. And a good excuse for going presented itself."

"What was that?"

"Rob's brother."

His eyes narrowed a little, with irony. "Did he want to marry you too?"

132

"I didn't stay long enough to find out," she replied composedly.

"I see. And so Nell was devastated to leave the Sedburghs." He sounded cool enough but Frances caught the sudden unguarded flicker of his eyelids. She spoke quickly, wanting to get it over with."

"It was not easy, of course. But she soon settled in here. And she had my father." She made a helpless gesture. "You know how he was with me, Ian. How he still is. Well, it is the same with Nell. He thinks she is perfect. He spoils her shamefully. She adores him."

" 'Poppy,' in fact, has taken the place of 'Papa,' " Ian said.

"Yes."

There was a long silence and then Ian asked, "What do you advise me to do, Frances? I do not relish the thought of my daughter hating me."

She winced slightly at what she heard in his voice. "She will come around, Ian. She is, basically, thank God, a very adaptable child. You must have patience, though."

And patience he certainly had, Frances thought as she watched him with Nell all during the week between their return from Loch Shiel and his departure for Inverary. Sir Donal had left for Edinburgh two days before Frances and Ian returned to Castle Hunter, so Nell has been left in the care of Ian's mother and sister. They both wore themselves out trying to entertain her, but when Frances came into the upstairs drawing room Nell had flung herself into her mother's arms like an abandoned child.

She stuck to Frances like a leech for the next few days, but since Frances spent most of her time with Ian the two were thrown together. He put aside all the affairs that were clamoring to be attended to and devoted himself to wooing his daughter. Together, he and Frances showed her all haunts of their own mutual childhood and made her laugh with the stories of the adventures they had had. Ian built a dam with her in a Highland stream, both of them getting extremely wet in the process. He let her help him row a boat. He taught her how to skip stones and how to climb a tree. Frances watched with a smile in her eyes as he won over their daughter the same way he had won her years ago. The reward for all his trouble came the day before he left. He came into the sitting room that adjoined Frances's bedroom where she was sorting through a box of books. Nell was with her, fidgeting around the window looking out at the mountains shimmering in the clear sun.

"I'm going fishing," he announced. "Do you care to come with me, Frances?"

She looked from him to Nell and then shook her head. "No, I want to finish unpacking these books. Then I promised to go over the house with your mother."

"Very well." He took a step toward the door and then turned to Nell. "Would you like to come fishing with me, Nell?"

"I've never been fishing," the little girl answered cautiously.

"I'll teach you," he responded promptly. "I taught your mother when she was a little girl. I always thought she was the only girl I'd ever go fishing with because she knows how to keep quiet." He frowned suddenly. "Do you think you could be quiet?" he asked anxiously.

Nell looked scornful. "Of course."

"That's all right then. Do you want to come?"

134

The child hesitated, looking at her mother for guidance. But Frances's face was expressionless. "It is up to you, Nell," she said. "You may go or stay, just as you please."

Nell wavered, obviously reluctant to leave the safety of Frances's side. But the promise of fishing and the blazing life in Ian's eyes were too strong a lure. "I think I'll go fishing," she said.

"Fine," replied Frances, careful to keep the relief from her voice. "Be sure you're back in time for dinner."

"Maybe I'll catch a fish for you to eat, Mama," said Nell excitedly.

"That would be fun, my love. There is nothing as good as fish from a Highland loch."

"I know," Nell said importantly, and Ian laughed.

"Get a jacket, Nell," he advised. "It can get chilly out on the water."

"All right. Wait for me, I'll be right back!" She darted out of the room and they could hear her running down the hall. They barely had a chance to exchange a glance of mutual congratulation before she was back with her jacket. Frances watched from the window as they left the castle together, and tears stung her eyes. Then, laughing at her own emotion, she returned to unpacking her books.

Ian rode by himself when he left for Inverary the next morning. His mother had wanted him to take a tail of gillies with him to demonstrate his importance, but he had refused. "I don't want any incidents, mother, and Lochaber Macdonalds do not mix well with the members of Clan Diarmed." This was indisputably true and so it was a solitary horseman who left Castle Hunter on that fine September morning. He rode through Glen Etive to the ferry on the northern shore of the beautiful loch of the same name where he was rowed across the quiet, blue water. He stopped at the hostelry on the other side for something to eat, then proceeded on his way toward Argyll through the Pass of Brander. Mighty Ben Cruachan towered above him on one side, and on the other was the deep black water of the Awe as it streamed toward Loch Etive. He stopped at the inn in Dalmally for a meal and then turned his horse south, toward Loch Fyne, the long sea loch at whose head stood Inverary Castle, ancient seat of Mac Caileinmhor, the Duke of Argyll, chief of the Campbells, the hated Clan Diarmed, the blood enemies of the Macdonalds of Lochaber.

The Duke was not in residence. Ian was received by his nephew, James Campbell of Ardkinglas. The Ardkinglas Campbells were from Loch Goil, a few miles to the east of Inverary and Loch Fyne. James Campbell had a fine estate of his own, but in his uncle's absence he came periodically to Inverary to consult with the Duke's factor and to send word to his uncle. It was morning, as Ian had spent the night in the inn in town. He had come to ask for Campbell help, but he did not want to be put in the position of having to ask for Campbell hospitality.

James Campbell was the same age as Ian and had been up at Cambridge with him, although at a different college. He had been profoundly surprised when the major-domo had announced the Earl of Lochaber. The Macdonalds of Lochaber had been for centuries the chief rivals and enemies of his clan. They were Catholic and Jacobite while the Campbells were Protestant and

Hanoverian. They could never rival the Campbells in wealth but their prestige among the Scottish nobility was enormous. People listened to the Campbells out of fear. They listened to the Macdonalds out of affection and pride. 'Loyal as Lochaber' was a saying heard not infrequently on the streets of Edinburgh. So it was an occasion of some magnitude that the Earl of Lochaber should present himself at Inverary Castle.

James Campbell told the major-domo to bring the Earl to him in the library and then stood looking at the door, a faint frown between his brows. He was, in fact, a little in awe of Ian Macdonald and was trying to conceal it as best he could.

To the older nobility of England and Scotland, Ian was an unknown quantity. To his peers who had been at school with him, he was a legend. At Eton he had been the best fighter in the school. Even in his first year the older boys had left him alone. And he had been un-equalled in sports. By the time he graduated he had been the acknowledged king of the school, followed wher-ever he went by a cluster of admiring satellites. It had been the same at Cambridge. Life just seemed more vivid and exciting around Ian. Very few refused to follow where he led. The final act that had rung down the curtain on his Cambridge career was still talked about among undergraduates five years after it had hap-pened. Campbell had heard men boast of having been in that race; it had gone down as one of the epic escapades in university history. The fact that Ian had been the only one expelled was a measure of how accurately the authorities had understood the power of his leadership. The race had gone unremarked in the world at large but

Campbell knew it was one of the landmarks of his own generation.

So now he stood waiting for Ian Macdonald, a trifle angry at himself for feeling the way he did. He remembered Ian as being larger than life, he told himself. Doubtless he would find that the reality fell far short of his schoolboy memory.

It didn't. If anything, the Earl of Lochaber was even more overwhelming than Campbell remembered. Ian filled the doorway, his dark eyes fixed interrogatively on James Campbell. "Ardkinglas?" he said in his deep, slow voice. "My business is with the Duke."

"My uncle is in London, Lord Lochaber," replied Campbell. "Perhaps I may be of assistance to you."

"Damn," said Ian and came into the room. He wore buckskin riding breeches, topboots, and a coat of blue superfine that fit perfectly across his broad shoulders. There was nothing in his attire to suggest that he was anything but a well-born English gentleman. His face gave the lie to the subdued fashion of his clothes. It was as Campbell remembered, full of strength and vivid life and the suggestion of suppressed violence. It was not precisely a handsome face, but it was one you did not forget. "Do you expect him to return anytime in the near future?" Ian asked the slender man who was dressed like himself in ordinary riding clothes. The kilt was no longer proscribed in Scotland, but very few wore it except on dress occasions.

"No. I believe he plans to remain in London for several months."

There was a silence as Ian looked speculatively at James Campbell, obviously trying to decide whether or not to deal with him in place of the absent duke.

Campbell's mouth tightened in annoyance. He did not like being made to feel insignificant. Ian's arrogance was all the more damning, he thought, because it was totally unconscious. "If I cannot help you, my lord," he said, an edge to his voice.

Ian had made up his mind. "You have lands not far from here, Ardkinglas, if I'm not mistaken"

"Yes."

"Are you bringing in sheep?"

"No, I am not."

"Good. If you can spare me a few minutes, Ardkinglas, I have a plan I should like to talk over with you."

"Certainly, my lord," said Campbell stiffly. "Won't you be seated?"

Forty minutes later he was looking at Ian with respect on his face. "It sounds like an excellent scheme to me," he said. "In fact, I might be interested in trying the same thing at Ardkinglas. We are not nearly so wealthy as Inverary, I'm afraid."

"No one is," said Ian ruefully, and Campbell laughed.

"You surprise me, my lord. I did not think to find in you an agrarian reformer." Ian's brows rose slightly, and in response to his unasked question Campbell continued, "I was at Cambridge the same time you were."

Ian grinned. "I take your point." He looked more closely at Campbell. "I don't think I remember you, Ardkinglas. Did we meet there?"

"I was at King's," James Campbell said in an expressionless tone. "We didn't meet." What he did not say was that a quiet, scholarly boy who bore the name of Campbell would hardly have dared to introduce himself to the notice of Ian Macdonald.

Ian nodded, satisfied by the spoken reply. His dark gaze looked appreciatively at the quiet figure before him. James Campbell was a good-looking young man with, the typical Campbell coloring of chestnut hair and blue eyes. His six feet of agile height was disposed casually in a comfortable chair, his long fingers idly tapping a letter opener against its arm. Ian liked the steady way the other man's eyes met his. "Do you think the duke would be interested?" he asked.

"Yes, I do." Campbell sat up a little straighter in his chair. "Can you go to London? The kind of backing you are looking for is best found there, you know. It would be easiest to see my uncle and then, if he agrees, see about negotiating a loan at the same time.

"I suppose I can." Ian smiled crookedly. But it's the devil of a time, Ardkinglas. I've not been married four weeks yet."

"Married?" James Campbell looked surprised. "I didn't know." There was a pause. "Perhaps you could take Lady Lochaber with you," he said tentatively.

Ian found himself feeling as reluctant as Robert Sedburgh had been to take Frances to London. "Perhaps."

"In my experience one rarely has difficulty in getting a woman to go to London," Campbell said good-humoredly. "At any rate I strongly suggest you go to see my uncle. In fact, I would be willing to speak to him myself on your behalf."

"Would you now?" Ian said slowly.

"Yes." Campbell leaned forward and his voice became tinged with definite enthusiasm. "The more I think about this scheme of yours, Lochaber, the more I like it. It would benefit the tenants economically and anything that brings more income in to them will naturally benefit us as landowners. Everyone would profit."

"*If* it works."

"If it works." Campbell's dark blue eyes held Ian's. "I think it will."

Ian smiled and, irresistibly, James Campbell smiled back. "I think it will too, Ardkinglas. I shall see you in London, then?"

Campbell rose. "You will. In three weeks' time?"

Ian held out his hand and James Campbell took it. It was a simple gesture but momentous in the history of their clans, and both men knew it. "You can get my direction from my cousin, Douglas Macdonald. He has a studio in Queen Anne's Gate. I don't know yet where I'll be staying. I'll have to talk to my wife; she is more familiar with London than I am."

"Oh, is Lady Lochaber English?"

"No." The brown eyes looked ironically at Campbell. "Perhaps you know her, Ardkinglas. Frances Stewart."

Campbell felt his jaw drop slightly and with an effort closed it again. "Frances Stewart? Do you mean Lady Robert Sedburgh?"

Ian did not care to hear Frances called by that name. "Yes," he said shortly.

"We were introduced once in Edinburgh," Ardkinglas said faintly, "but I doubt she would remember me."

"Well, I will introduce you again in London." Ian then firmly refused all offers of hospitality by saying he hoped to make it home that day, and James Campbell watched his tall, broad-shouldered figure leave the room as easily and arrogantly as he had entered it. Campbell's eyes were narrowed as he sat down slowly again in his chair. Then he laughed out loud and shook his head in admiration. Trust Ian Macdonald to come home and calmly walk off with the most sought-after woman in Britain, he thought. Perhaps the legend had not been wrong, after all.

Chapter Seventeen

My hairt is subject, bound and thrall
—ALEXANDER SCOTT

Frances was supremely happy. She had forgotten how it was to feel this way. During the week she went about with a light step, soft-spoken and patient and joyful in all her undertakings. She and Ian's mother had no difficulty in coming to terms. The Dowager had spoken seriously to Frances before the marriage and told her she had intended to take a house for herself and Margaret in Edinburgh. Frances had answered readily, "I think that would be a good idea, Godmama. That way if you ever feel the need to get away from us you'll have some place to go. And you will be able to entertain at your own pleasure. But if you plan to abandon Castle Hunter for Edinburgh permanently I shall be extremely distressed."

Lady Lochaber had said bluntly, "It never works out, Frances, this sharing of a house. Look at the Dunkelds."

"My dear ma'am," said Frances with real warmth, "I am not Mary Dunkeld and *you* are not the Dowager

Lady Dunkeld. There is certainly enough to do in Castle Hunter for the two of us to keep busy and out of each other's way.''

As Lady Lochaber really had not wanted to leave her home she allowed Frances to talk her into staying and the result seemed to be satisfactory to all parties. When Frances and Ian had returned from Loch Shiel they had found the master bedroom suite vacated and prepared for them. The earl's room had been empty since the death of Ian's father; Lady Lochaber had always told Charlie she had no intention of removing until he married. So now the two connecting bedrooms and adjoining sitting room were prepared and ready for the new Earl of Lochaber and his countess.

It had not taken Ian's mother and his wife long to arrange the household responsibilities. Frances had lived at Aysgarth for three years with a mother-in-law with whom she had not the childhood ties that she had to her godmother. They were both anxious to get along with each other and had mutual affection and respect to act as the foundation for their new relationship. They managed extremely well.

The day after Ian had left for Inverary Nell went about looking slightly lost and lonely. That evening as Frances was reading a book to her before putting her to bed she brought up a subject that had been on her mind for a few days. ''Mama,'' she said in the middle of her favorite story, ''what am I supposed to call Ian?''

They were sitting in the upstairs drawing room and Margaret was there as well, working on some embroidery. The two women's eyes met briefly and then Frances said ''What do you mean, darling?''

''Well, I can't call him Papa; my papa is dead.

Should I call him Ian like you do, Mama? Only Nurse told me it was rude for me to call grownups by their Christian names."

This was a question that had been perplexing Frances as well, and she had not come to any satisfactory conclusion. As she hesitated in answering Margaret said, "Ian and I always called my father 'Dada,' Nell. I know Ian would be pleased to have you call him that if you feel you'd like to."

" 'Dada,' " said Nell experimentally. She looked at Frances.

"I think that would be just fine, Nell. What do you think?"

"I like it," the little girl said. "It sounds Highland."

Margaret laughed. "It is."

"Finish the story, Mama," Nell said impatiently. Her problem solved, she was anxious to return to her evening ritual.

"All right, all right," said Frances and her smiling eyes met Margaret's in a brief glance of gratitude before she turned once again to her daughter's book.

Frances went upstairs early that evening. It had begun to rain, but as she did not expect Ian until tomorrow at the earliest she was not concerned. She let her maid brush her hair and help her undress and then dismissed her for the night. After the door closed behind the maid Frances was drawn irresistibly to the window. Ever since childhood she had loved to listen to the rain at night. On impulse she threw open the window and shivered as the cool, wet air poured into the room. She got her warm robe from the wardrobe and pulled a chair around so it was only a few feet away from and facing

145

the window. Then she curled up comfortably, her eyes on the rain as it drummed on the windowsill.

She was not aware Ian was home until she heard the door to the room next to hers open. She knew his step instantly. Then she could hear him moving around, the deep tones of his voice as he spoke to his valet. She stayed where she was until she heard the connecting door between their rooms open and then she turned her head. "I didn't expect you tonight. You must have gotten drenched."

"I did," he replied. "It's much nicer to be in here looking out." He walked across the room to where she sat and stood for a moment looking down at her. Her hair had been plaited for the night and fell in a braid as thick as his wrist over her shoulder. It looked very pale against the crimson velvet of her robe. Her eyes were wide and mysterious as they gazed up at him. "I missed you," he said, and, picking her up, sat down in the chair with her in his lap.

Frances rested her cheek against the broad shoulder of his dressing gown. "How did it go?" she asked softly.

"Argyll wasn't there. I talked to his nephew. Campbell of Ardkinglas. He seemed to think the duke would be interested." He didn't want to tell Frances tonight of the necessity of going to London.

"Good." Frances too did not want to talk. They sat together in silence for perhaps ten more minutes, Ian's cheek against her hair. Then he stood up, set her on her feet and went to close the window. He turned back. "Come, mo chridhe," he said in Gaelic. "Let us go to bed."

*   *   *

Later, as Ian slept beside her, his arm heavy across her breast, Frances lay awake still listening to the rain. She felt as though there were a spell on her; as if Ian had carried her straight from the small cottage in Surrey where first he had made love to her to this room tonight. It seemed as though she must have lain in his arms and dreamed the long years in between. The rain tonight was the selfsame rain as then and the five lost years were as nothing. She moved a little closer to him in the bed and in a few minutes she too was asleep.

The next morning over breakfast, which they took together in Frances's sitting room, he told her in detail of his visit. "Oh, Ian," she wailed. "I hate the thought of dragging off to London now."

He buttered a piece of toast. "You don't have to come if you don't want to."

She stared at him. "Are you out of your mind? Do you think I'm going to turn you loose in London by yourself? Of course I'm coming."

He cocked an eyebrow at her but held his peace. "Where do you suggest we stay, Frances? I told Ardkinglas to apply to Douglas for our direction."

She looked thoughtful. "We can't stay at a hotel," she murmured. "It wouldn't be at all suitable for Nell."

"Nell!"

"Yes, Nell. You certainly don't think we can dump her here on your mother and take off for London for a few months."

"My mother won't mind."

"Nell will," said Frances uncompromisingly. "She'll kick up a fuss about leaving because she is having fun, but she would be far more distressed if we left her. Then she *would* hate you."

There was a little silence, then, "I see what you mean," Ian said.

"Good. Furthermore, I think we should take Margaret."

Ian stared at his wife's serene face as she poured herself a cup of coffee. "You do?"

"Yes. She is a beautiful girl, Ian, and she deserves to meet some interesting men. Most definitely she should come with us."

"How about my mother? And your father? And of course there's always Angus the gardener. He might feel left out if we neglected to take him as well."

Frances gave him an enchanting smile. "Don't be sarcastic, Ian. Surely you see that we should take Margaret?"

Very few people were proof against that smile. "Oh, all right," he said resignedly. "But to get back to my original question—where shall we stay?"

"Well I always stayed at Aysgarth House before," said Frances reflectively, "but I hardly think it would be possible to do that under the present circumstances." She looked up from stirring her coffeee, a mischievous glint in her eyes, and was startled by the suddenly grim expression that had come over Ian's features. "I think we should hire a house for a few months," she said hastily. "I'm sure Douglas can find something for us. Why don't you write to him, Ian? That way we'll have a house when we arrive."

There was a pause. "Very well," he said finally. "I suppose that would be best. Have you any idea what this little venture is likely to cost me?"

"Enough. Houses in London don't come cheap."

She bit her lip, then said, "Why don't you let me help, Ian? I have money. I could pay for the London trip."

"We have been over this before, Frances," he replied evenly. "Your money is yours, for you and for Nell. I won't touch a penny of it."

"You didn't feel like that five years ago," she said stubbornly.

"We were talking then about your mother's money. The money you inherited from Sedburgh is quite another matter."

"I don't see why where it came from should make any difference. It is mine now."

He gave her a long tight-lipped stare. "I don't care to discuss it any further."

"Very well," she replied stiffly. "If you want to be pigheaded go ahead. But it is there for you to use should you ever need it."

"I won't."

"No," she replied with a trace of bitterness. "I don't suppose you will."

Chapter Eighteen

Albeid I knaw
Of luvis law
The plessur and the panis smart
—ALEXANDER SCOTT

They traveled to Perth and from there to London by boat. Ian had been horrified by the amount of baggage that Frances accumulated for the trip. "I moved whole armies with less equipment than that," he said to her while staring in fascinated horror at the luggage being loaded on the carriage.

She had giggled at the expression on his face. "You're a married man now, and a father, my love. Life will never be the same again I'm afraid."

He shook his head. "I can see that."

But he made no more complaints. He had become completely reconciled to taking Nell the moment she had swung from his hands and called him "Dada." To the deep delight of his wife, mother, and sister he was rapidly becoming like wax in the little girl's hands.

"She is going to be a terror when she grows up,"

Frances confided to Margaret. "She certainly knows how to manage men."

Margaret laughed. "She must get it from her mother," she retorted unsympathetically. Frances had simply raised her eyebrows and gone off to supervise some more packing.

They arrived in London three weeks and two days after Ian's conversation with James Campbell of Ardkinglas. They went first to Grillon's Hotel where Frances, Margaret, and Nell gratefully sank into wide, comfortable beds. Ian left to seek out Douglas.

His cousin was at home, working in his studio. It was the first time the two had met since Ian had returned from South America. They talked for half an hour before they got round to the topic that had brought Ian to London. "I rented you a house in Mount Street," Douglas said. "It belongs to Sir Horace Cherney, but he is spending the next few months on the Continent, so it was available. The staff comes with it, so you won't have to worry about engaging people."

"Excellent, Douglas." Ian put down his glass of wine and asked cautiously, "How much?"

The price was surprisingly reasonable. "I know Sir Horace rather well," explained Douglas. He frowned. "Are you strapped for money, Ian?"

"Somewhat. The problem is that I need rather a lot of capital. I'm going into the sheep-farming business."

"What!"

"Don't look at me like that, Douglas. It is not what you think. I'm not going to evict anyone. But I do want to break up the maze of small crofts that covers Lochaber. They hardly provide subsistence living for the tenants.

152

Sheep, on the other hand, have proved to be profitable. What I would like to do is fall back on the old clan tradition of cooperative labor and create sheep farms to be run by groups of crofters. Everyone would contribute something to the capital and labor required to run them, and all would share mutually in the profits.''

Douglas was looking at his cousin, an odd expression on his face. "And what would your role be?"

"Well, since the land belongs to me the crofters would have to pay me rent. I foresee that in the future I will make rather a decent profit."

"And for the present?"

Ian smiled crookedly. "For the present I pay. As there will be no wealthy Lowlander to bring in his sheep and pay me high rents for emptying Lochaber I shall have to foot the bill myself."

"Buy the sheep you mean?"

"Yes. And support the crofters for a little bit. And pay for transport to the market. It will take more capital than I've got."

"What are you going to do?" Douglas was blunt.

So was Ian. "Ask the Duke of Argyll to cosign a bank loan with me."

There was a stunned silence. "Argyll?" said Douglas.

"Argyll. He is no friend to the clearances. He has the money and the prestige to stand behind me. There is no other Highland chief who can do it; the rest of them are even poorer than I am. So I am going to ask the Duke. That, my dear cousin, is the reason I came to London."

"Sweet Jesus." Douglas blinked several times rapidly. "The world must be coming to an end."

Ian looked grimly amused. "I can't say it is a popular idea with my family but, as I said to Frances, I learned in South American that the nation who refuses to mend its own internal disputes in the face of a common threat is a nation on the verge of destruction."

"Yes," Douglas said slowly, "I see your point." He looked at Ian and for the first time said her name, "How does Frances feel about all this?"

"Oh, she agrees with me." Ian grinned ruefully. "Frances has never been a very good hater. My mother and sister, now, they have the true Macdonald spirit when it comes to the Campbells. They are very disturbed about this. But they are realists as well. They had no other suggestion to put forward so they have screwed their courage to the sticking point and reluctantly agreed. I'm sure they both secretly hope Mac Caileinmhor will spit in my face so they can go back to hating him with impunity."

Douglas threw back his head and laughed. "You are probably right." He sobered suddenly and said with uncharacteristic intensity. "I hope it all goes well, Ian."

"So do I," Ian replied just as soberly. "So do I."

The house in Mount Street proved to be just what Frances had had in mind. The nursery was not furnished but Nell settled quite happily into a bedroom not far removed from her mother's. Once she had gotten organized Frances sat down to write a few notes. One was to her aunt, Lady Mary Grahan, whom she believed to be in residence in Hanover Square. The other was to the Earl and Countess of Aysgarth in Kent, telling them that she was in London with Nell.

The next thing Frances did was take her sister-in-law shopping. "This is my treat," she said firmly to Margaret's protestations. "If I am going to take you to parties

154

and introduce you to people you must be properly dressed. As a matter of fact I had better buy some clothes myself. Edinburgh fashions are always a year behind London's.''

Lady Mary came to visit, delighted to see Frances and full of plans for introducing Margaret to as many eligible men as possible. Margaret tended to be rather wary of all these plans. She was not anxious to marry some ''mincing Sassenach,'' as she said to Frances.

''You don't have to marry anybody,'' Frances replied calmly. ''Just have a good time. There is the theater and the opera and concerts—all kinds of entertainment that I know you will enjoy. I imagine Ian will want to be home for Christmas so we may as well see and do as much as we can in the few months we have. Winter in the Highlands must be rather quiet.''

Frances's words made sense to Margaret. She had the Macdonald zest for living and determined to enjoy her stay in London to the utmost. As she also had the Macdonald scorn for the English she pushed the idea of marriage right out of her mind. When Margaret married it would be to one of her own kind.

One of their first visitors in Mount Street was Douglas. He had found himself reluctant to go but could discover no excuse for staying away. Margaret greeted him in the drawing room. ''You look marvelous, Margaret,'' he told her, surveying with approval her tall slender figure clad in a walking dress of dusty rose.

''Thank you, Douglas. Frances's doing, of course. The only problem is that I have to make most of my appearances with her by my side. It doesn't seem to have occurred to her that her presence is a distinct disadvantage to her precious scheme of making me the toast of London.'' Margaret's dark eyes were full of affectionate laughter. Despite her words the prospect of making her debut under Frances's aegis did not appear to be disturbing to her at all.

''Nonsense. You will complement each other. And dark beauties are all the fashion at the moment, I might add.''

There was a sound in the hall and Douglas turned to see Frances coming in the door. He would know her light step anywhere, he thought. He stood holding her hand and thinking, I had forgotten she could look this way. The fire within her that had gone out five years ago when Ian left was lit again. He had never even realized that what they all had been seeing in the interim was simply the glow of the embers. She smiled her unbelievable smile. ''Thank you so much, Douglas, for finding us this house. Perhaps if you weren't so utterly efficient we all wouldn't rely on you so outrageously.''

His kind face was surprisingly stern. ''I was happy to be able to help.''

Frances gestured him to a chair, seated herself and Margaret, and rang for tea. He was still sitting there half an hour later when Ian came in. Frances looked at her husband, and her eyes were indescribably beautiful. ''You look as if you've had good news,'' she said to him.

His own eyes glinted and he came across the room to where she sat. Douglas watched the arrogant, lazy grace of that big body as it bent over Frances briefly. For a moment his lips tightened, then he heard what Ian was saying. ''You were successful?'' he asked incredulously.

''Yes. I just spent two hours with Mac Caileinmhor. He has agreed to stand behind me.''

156

"I never had any fears he would not," said Frances with serene radiance.

Ian's hand went out very briefly to touch her knee. "You're prejudiced."

"Well I'm glad you are all happy," Margaret said bitterly. "I find it a bit more difficult to be beholden to the Campbells."

"Pride is a dangerous luxury, Maggie," Ian said gravely. At this his sister, his wife, and his cousin all turned to stare in astonishment. He was serious. They looked in silence at his dark face with its brilliant eyes, high cheekbones, strong nose, and proud mouth. Then, in unison, they began to laugh. "May I ask what you find so amusing?" Ian inquired.

"You. Preaching humility!" Margaret recovered her breath first.

After a moment Ian grinned, taking in the still-convulsed faces of his wife and cousin. "I see what you mean. But all the same, Maggie, I mean it. I'm not asking you to love the Campbells. Even I would find that an impossibility. But we can be civil and cooperative with each other. The Duke is going to Ireland for a month, so he has delegated his nephew Ardkinglas to work out the arrangements with me. He seems a decent sort of chap."

"For a Campbell," said Margaret.

"For a Campbell," he agreed. "You don't have to see much of him, Maggie, but if you are rude to him I'll murder you."

Margaret's mouth set and Frances said gently, "Of course we will be pleasant to Mr. Campbell. Won't we, Margaret?"

Margaret looked at the beautiful, slightly austere face of her sister-in-law and sighed. "Oh, all right. I'll be nice to Mr. Bloody Campbell. If it kills me."

"It won't kill you, Maggie love," said Ian. "I'm sure of it."

Chapter Nineteen

And fair Marg'ret, and rare Marg'ret,
   And Marg'ret o' veritie,
Gin ere ye love another man
   N'er love him as ye did me.

         — ANONYMOUS

The Macdonalds' arrival in London created a considerable stir among the ton. Frances, of course, had a number of friends whom she had seen regularly during the years of her widowhood. She also had an impressive number of disappointed suitors who flocked to bemoan their fate and see if she really seemed to be happy with Lochaber. "She married him after all," was the consensus of those who remembered that summer five years ago when Frances and Ian had been the chief gossip tidbits at everyone's dinner table.

Frances was used to the ways of London and paid scant attention to the curiosity watchers whose eyes were constantly on her. In truth, she had been something of a celebrity for so long that she really was oblivious to the stir her presence invariably caused.

Ian, on the contrary, was startled to find himself the center of as much attention as he was accorded. In Scotland he expected to be deferred to; in England he was an unknown. The Lochabers did not even sit in the House of Lords.

What had happened was that society was now filled with the young men who had been at school with him. Ian found himself somewhat cynically amused to be suddenly famous because he had been the terror of Eton and Cambridge. He was far from regarding his schooldays with the wistful nostalgia that seemed to afflict so many of his peers. He had been champing at the bit to leave the whole time he was there and he cherished no desire to return to the playing fields of his boyhood glory.

To add to his past legend, however, he now had the glamorous distinction of his years in South America. And the publication of *Waverly* had raised to fever pitch the English interest in the romantic Scottish Highlands. London was in the mood to appreciate a Highland chieftain from an intensely Jacobite family who looked, as one young lady said soulfully, ''Just like Conrad in Lord Byron's *Corsair*.''

Ian, however, was engaged in far more mundane affairs than Byron's heroes ever sullied their hands with. He and James Campbell spent a great deal of time working out the details of the arrangement that was to exist between Lochaber and Argyll. Ian also spent time with the secretary of the Venezuelan legation, Andrés Bello, and he had several conversations with the foreign secretary Lord Castlereagh about the war in South America.

Margaret was unaffectedly enjoying herself and the reflected glory of her brother and sister-in-law. She went to balls and danced, she went to dinners and talked, she went to concerts and plays and listened. Her path, however, never crossed that of James Campbell of Ardkinglas until a few weeks after their arrival in London.

Campbell had called in Mount Street to keep an appointment with Ian. As Ian had not come in yet, Frances had told the butler to bring Mr. Campbell to her in the morning parlor. They had met on one previous occasion and Frances was inclined to like the slender, well-bred Scotsman with the steady blue eyes. They were chatting comfortably when the door opened and Margaret came in. "Oh, I beg your pardon, Frances," she said in her slow voice that in phrasing was so like her brother's. "I didn't realize you had company."

"Come in, Margaret," Frances replied, "and let me introduce Mr. James Campbell of Ardkinglas to you." Frances cast a hasty glance at the man who had risen immediately upon Margaret's entrance and what she saw on his face shook her profoundly. She looked back quickly at Margaret, who was standing a few paces into the room. Her tall, slim figure was still as a statue, her brown eyes under the dark, finely arched brows were staring directly into the eyes of James Campbell. She looked spellbound. Holy, Mother, thought Frances, this can't be happening.

For a breathless moment no one spoke, then faint color stained Margaret's clear olive skin. "What did you say?" she asked Frances with palpable effort.

"I said I should like to introduce Mr. James Campbell."

The beautiful color drained from Margaret's face. She stared at Frances with appalled eyes. "Did you say Campbell?"

"Yes."

"I—see. How do you do, Mr. Campbell," she said to the intense blue eyes of the man staring at her as if he had seen a vision. "I just looked in to see if you want something from the lending library, Frances," she added hastily.

"No, thank you anyway," Frances returned.

"Very well. I'm off, then," said Margaret, and retreated swiftly from the room.

Frances turned slowly to face James Campbell of Ardkinglas. He had flushed darkly red. "Who was that?" he asked Frances in a taut voice.

"Good heavens," said Frances, really shaken now. "Didn't I say? That was my sister-in-law, Margaret Macdonald."

"Lochaber's sister?"

"Yes."

"Oh." There was a pause then he said flatly, "She doesn't much care for the Campbells, I take it."

Frances's eyes dropped to her hands, which were slowly folding a piece of embroidery over and over. "She is a Macdonald of Lochaber and Glencoe. It is a clan that has a long memory."

"Yes, I know." There was a moment of strained silence and then the door opened and Ian came in. He sensed the unease, took in the somber look on Campbell's face, the tenseness of Frances's body, and frowned. "Is anything wrong?"

"Of course not," Frances said too quickly and Campbell seconded her eagerly. By unspoken mutual consent neither said anything about Margaret. In a few minutes Ian led Ardkinglas away to the library and Frances was left alone in the morning parlor. She knew what it was she had just seen. Frances was a firm believer in love at first sight. It had happened to her when she was a great deal younger than Margaret. But like her sister-in-law she was appalled at who were the parties involved. Ian wouldn't like it. Of that she was positive. Even Frances found her mind shying away from the thought of marriage to a Campbell. And what, for the love of heaven, must Margaret be thinking?

A second confrontation occurred that week to disturb the accord of the Lochaber household. The Earl and Countess of Aysgarth came to town and Frances took Nell to see them. She had been slightly apprehensive about their reaction to her marriage but they seemed to be genuinely pleased for her. "After all," as Lady Aysgarth had said to her husband when they first received the news, "it has been two years since Robert's death. One could hardly expect a beautiful young woman like Frances to remain a widow forever." The only fear that the Aysgarths had was that they would lose touch with Nell.

"Of course you will continue to see her," Frances had said warmly when she divined this concern. "Why you know how Nell loves her Grandmama and Grandpapa." And when Lady Aysgarth asked if Nell could return with them to Kent for two weeks Frances had not been able to say no. She was acutely aware that from Ian's point of view it was not the time to bring in the Sedburghs, but he would have to accept their relationship to Nell one day. So she said yes, to Nell's delight; her grandparents spoiled her shamefully and she reveled in it.

Frances and Margaret were going to the theater with a party that evening and Ian was engaged with some South American friends, so he was not going to accompany

163

them. He came into Frances's dressing room before he left to say goodbye, and she dismissed her maid and said, "I have something to tell you, Ian, and I'd better do it before you hear it from Nell."

He sat down in a fragile chair and Frances offered a silent prayer that it wouldn't break under him. "What is happening?" he asked.

"I went to see the Aysgarths today," she said quietly. "They arrived in London this week."

At the name Aysgarth Ian's face had hardened. "Oh?" he said only.

"Yes. I took Nell." He said nothing and after a moment she went on, conscious that her heart was beating uncomfortably fast. "They wanted to take Nell to Aysgarth with them for two weeks and I said she could go."

Ian's mouth looked like it was set in iron. "No," he said.

Frances had promised herself never to quarrel with Ian again, but on this subject she knew she could not give in. "Why not?" she asked steadily. "Surely you are not so small-minded that you can't share Nell with two old people who love her?"

It was not Nell that Ian found it impossible to share but he could hardly say that to Frances. How could he explain the fact that he was jealous of a dead man? The shadow of Robert Sedburgh had been hovering over him ever since they arrived in London. "After all, Ian," he heard Frances say, "they are her grandparents."

He rose to his feet, intimidatingly large in that delicate, woman's room. "*They are not her grandparents*," he said with harsh emphasis.

She stared at him, her face taking on that remote look

164

it wore when she was angry. "They don't know that."

He suddenly took a step toward her. "How did they know you were in town?" he asked grimly.

She didn't drop her eyes. "I wrote to tell them, of course."

Ian suddenly bent his head so that his eyes were shielded from her. "You just can't let him go, can you?" he asked softly. Then, as Frances stared at him in utter stupefaction, he looked up and his face was a stranger's mask. "Do what you want with Nell," he said in a clipped voice. "You will anyway no matter what I say." And he walked out of the room.

Frances sat in bewildered silence which slowly smoldered into anger the more she thought about what he had said. Little did Ian care about her loyalties and her obligations. He had never forgiven her for not telling him about Nell. That was clear to her now. Well, if he thought he was going to just erase four years out of Nell's life he was mistaken. With bitterness in her heart, Frances summoned her maid and finished dressing for the theater.

Chapter Twenty

To luve unluvit it is ane pane
                                        —ALEXANDER SCOTT

Frances did not enjoy her theater party that evening. She and Margaret had been invited to share the box of the Earl of Carstairs, a Scot who was very influential in English society. He was thirty years of age, unmarried, good looking, and wealthy. Frances did not think it would hurt to give Margaret the opportunity to become better acquainted with him. Unfortunately her plans did not include the presence of James Campbell.

He came into the box a few minutes before the play began and Frances felt Margaret stiffen beside her. They exchanged a few brief pleasantries and then the lights dimmed and everyone's eyes turned to the stage. However, even Edmund Kean's demonically energetic Richard III could not keep the attention of three of the watchers in the Earl of Carstairs's box.

Margaret sat like a statue, but Frances was not fooled by that quiet composure. And James Campbell on the other side of her was equally tense. From time to time he glanced from the stage to Margaret. There was something in the straight lines of her profile that caused his hands to close hard on the edge of the box. When the intermission came he turned and said immediately, "Would you care to take a stroll into the lobby, Miss Macdonald?"

"Yes," said Margaret, and without further words the two of them left the box. Frances frowned slightly but made no attempt to follow them.

Lord Carstairs was not at all displeased to be left with Frances, and after a few minutes his box filled with the usual collection of her friends and admirers. Margaret and Campbell returned a few minutes before the curtain rose again. She looked pale but calm, and the rest of the evening passed in relatively easy accord.

Frances slept later than usual the next morning and as soon as she got up she was assailed by a wave of nausea. She quickly got back into bed and lay quietly, feeling the sickness slowly subside. She drifted back to sleep, and when she awoke two hours later she felt fine. She dressed slowly, an abstracted expression on her face. This was the fifth day this had occurred, and the stirrings of hope she had resolutely been beating down were now too strong to ignore. She was almost sure she was with child.

Uppermost in her emotions was relief. She had lived with Robert Sedburgh for two years after Nell's birth and she had never conceived. She had begun to be afraid that she never would; that God was punishing her for her sin with Ian. Rob had laughed when she told him this and said not to worry, they would have children in time. Frances, who very much wanted to give him a son to make up for all her own shortcomings, had not been so confident.

But this morning's queasiness was too familiar for her to disregard any longer. She had had it only once before. That, and the unusual sleepiness she had been experiencing lately. She was going to have a baby. Her heart swelled and she yearned with dizzy tenderness toward the time when she would once more hold an infant in her arms, feel the downy softness of its fragile head under her lips. She smiled radiantly. How pleased Ian would be.

At this point in her imaginings she came thumping uncomfortably back to earth. The memory of her last encounter with him was unpleasantly clear. She had been bitterly angry with him and he with her. But she could not harbor anger in her heart now. She was anchored to Ian by ties far stronger than the strongest chain; ties that she could not cut without breaking herself in two. Why fight him, then? She would put her resentment behind her and, when she told him of the coming baby, he would do the same.

Frances went down to lunch feeling comfortably hungry and looking forward to meeting her husband. When he didn't appear she was not overly disturbed and she made plans to go shopping with Margaret. When Margaret asked if she were feeling well she replied composedly, "Oh, yes. Just a trifle tired. I need to sleep later in London than I do at home."

Margaret was preoccupied with her own thoughts and did not notice anything odd in Frances, who had always had the energy of a young lioness, confessing that a few parties had tired her out. Margaret had had a very interesting conversation with James Campbell of Ardkinglas that morning at Hookham's lending library, and she was looking forward to seeing him at Lady Cowper's ball that evening. She had too many problems of her own at the moment to worry about her sister-in-law. Consequently they dropped Nell and her nurse at Aysgarth House and then spent an abstracted but busy afternoon at the Pantheon Bazaar.

Ian was not home for dinner either and arrived only to change into evening dress in time to escort his wife and sister to the Cowpers' ball. His face was hard and unyielding and his eyes did not soften as he regarded Frances, breathtaking in a gown of water green Italian silk with an opera comb set behind the heavy knot of ash-blonde hair on the crown of her head. She smiled at him tentatively but he said only, "I'm sorry to be late. Let's go." Then he looked at her again as he held her cloak and frowned. "Isn't that dress rather low cut?"

She looked surprised. "For Edinburgh perhaps, but for London it is really quite conservative."

He stared for a minute at the beautiful curve of her breasts, discreetly revealed by the scooped neckline of green silk. He shrugged. "If you want to show yourself to the world it's your affair I suppose. I can't say I like it."

Her long green eyes narrowed with dawning temper. "You never did have any taste in clothes," she said sweetly, took her cloak from his hands and walked out of the room.

The ride in the coach to the Cowpers' was distinctly uncomfortable. Margaret chatted gamely but got little assistance from either of her companions and at last she gave it up. As soon as they arrived Ian disappeared in the direction of the card room, Frances was claimed by four different men, and Margaret agreed to dance with James Campbell.

About half way through the evening Ian appeared with the Condessa de Losada, a Spanish widow who had been enlivening London society for the past several months. The Condessa was about thirty years of age, with a voluptuous figure, heavy-lidded brown eyes, and a full, sensual mouth. Any man who looked at her immediately thought of one thing only, but she had remained surprisingly elusive for one so obviously tantalizing. There was talk of a liaison between her and the Duke of Leyburn, but no one was certain of their exact relationship. She had been in Sussex for the past month, so this was the first time her path had crossed the Lochabers'.

"Who is that?" Frances asked Douglas, who was waiting to partner her in the next set.

Douglas looked. "That is the Condessa de Losada," he replied. "She is the widow of a rich Spaniard and has been gracing our shores for a few months now."

As they watched, Ian smiled down at the Condessa and, putting a hand on her waist, led her onto the floor.

"Well!" said Frances, indignation trembling in her voice. "And to think he had the audacity to make nasty comments about my neckline! If hers were any lower she'd fall out of it."

There was certainly a great deal of the luscious Condessa on view, but Ian didn't appear to be at all scandalized. The Condessa gave him a smile that could only be labelled seductive, and he bent his head to murmur something in her ear.

The waltz music started and Douglas lightly clasped

Frances around the waist and swung her into the dance. He could feel the tenseness of her body as they went round the room. "What's the matter?" he asked gently. "Surely you're not upset because Ian is dancing with the Condessa?"

"Upset?" Green panther's eyes looked into his. "Of course I'm not upset. What a silly thing to say, Douglas."

"I beg your pardon," he replied automatically, but a faint furrow appeared between his brows. When Frances looked like this she made him extremely nervous.

His apprehension was not allayed as the evening progressed. Ian appeared to be engrossed by the Condessa, who was making the most blatant bid for a man's attention that anyone had ever seen her make. Frances did not seem to be concerned, but there was a wintry remoteness about her that Douglas did not like at all. She spent half an hour in serious conversation with James Campbell of Ardkinglas, but otherwise her behavior appeared to be perfectly normal. However, she came up to him as everyone was going into supper and asked if he would take her home.

"What about Margaret?" he asked, although that was not the question that was on his mind.

"My aunt is here. She will keep an eye on Margaret. I hate to drag her away so early but I am really very tired."

She did look tired, Douglas thought. The skin under her eyes had a faint bluish cast, and though she walked as uprightly as ever it appeared to be an effort for her. "Are you all right, Frances?" he asked anxiously.

"I am fine. Just tired. Will you take me home, Douglas?"

"Of course. Wait here and I'll get your cloak." She

gave him a shadowy smile and gratefully sank down on a chair of gilt wood. She was so tired she was dizzy with it. It had come over her during the last half hour, an exhaustion so all-encompassing that it even doused the flames of her anger at Ian. But she would not ask him to take her home. It was with enormous gratitude that she saw Douglas returning with her cloak. "Dear Douglas," she murmured. "Where would I ever be without your kindness?"

Douglas's jaw clenched tightly as they went down the front stairs. He put her in the coach and then got in himself, giving the Mount Street direction to the driver. Her head was leaned back against the upholstery and her eyes were closed. "Frances," he said urgently. "Are you sure you aren't ill?"

"I'm quite sure." She opened her eyes and smiled reassuringly at him.

He left her in the front hall of her house and got back into the coach he had borrowed to return to the Cowpers'. It wasn't fair, he thought angrily, that she could still do this to him. She was in trouble. He knew it. And he still could not bear to see her unhappy. It had been like this for as long as he could remember. Ian. His anger suddenly burned hot against his cousin. What the hell was the matter with Ian?

Ian himself wasn't quite sure what was wrong with him. He only knew that suddenly he was desperately jealous of Frances. She had always attracted men as honey attracts flies and it had never bothered him before. Now it did.

He saw her go out with Douglas and abruptly abandoned his Condessa to get himself a drink, which he

173

took back into the card room. He stood by the window, gazing out at the London street, and his thoughts were not pleasant. Frances had spent a long time with that Campbell fellow, he thought. They had both looked very serious. What could they have been discussing?

He took a long swallow of champagne. The problem, he thought bitterly, was that he was no longer sure that Frances loved him. He had never been jealous before because he had always known that no one else mattered to Frances but him. It had been the rock-bottom certainty of his life—her love for him and his for her. But that certainty existed no longer.

She still loved Robert Sedburgh. He was almost sure of it. It was why she refused to let Nell break her ties to the Aysgarths. It was why she refused to allow him to give Nell his name. His sister's words came back to him: "She never talks about her husband, but I'm afraid she thinks about him." Ian was afraid of that also.

It gnawed at him. He knew he should take what she had to give him and be grateful for it but he couldn't. He couldn't be certain of her. She had married him because of Nell, and who knew when she would come to regret it? When she would once again turn from him to someone else, someone who, like Sedburgh, was all that he was not?

"Ian!" Douglas's voice interrupted his thoughts and he turned, an expression of such brooding bitterness on his face that Douglas was startled. "I took Frances home," he said after a moment. "She said she was tired, but I don't think she looked well."

174

"I see. Thank you, Douglas." Douglas hesitated a moment before the rock-hard mask of his cousin's face, then he shrugged, turned, and left Ian standing alone by the window.

Chapter Twenty-one

O waly, waly, gin love be bonnie
A little time while it is new!
But when 'tis auld it waxeth cauld,
And fades awa' like morning dew.

—ANONYMOUS

Ian and Margaret returned home a little after two that evening. Ian let his valet help him undress, then dismissed him. He hesitated for a moment, then quietly opened the connecting door between his room and Frances's and went in. She was deeply asleep, turned a little on one side, her face on her arm like a child. He was stepping back to return to his own room when she stirred slightly and opened her eyes. "Ian?" she asked in a voice foggy with sleep.

"Yes. I'm sorry I woke you but Douglas said you weren't feeling well."

She rolled over and pushed her hair off her cheek. "I'm all right. I was just tired."

"Then go back to sleep. I'm sorry I disturbed you."

But he didn't move away, just stood there looking at her, his head bent so that his dark hair swung forward and the light from the candle he carried slid over the line of his cheek, spiked now with the shadow of his lowered black lashes. She smiled at him sleepily and then yawned. He took a step back toward the bed and said, "What were you and Ardkinglas talking about for so long tonight?"

Dear God, thought Frances blinking at him in astonishment, how did he ever notice that conversation? She had thought he was too busy with the Condessa. The Condessa. At that Frances sat up in bed, her back ramrod straight. "I might ask you what you were doing drooling all over that half-naked Spaniard."

"Don't be ridiculous, Frances," he said irritably.

"Ridiculous!" She felt tears sting her eyes and angrily she dashed her hand against her cheeks. "I'm not the one who looked ridiculous."

Ian stared at her in surprise, irritation turning to concern. She was clearly upset. Frances never cries, he thought as he sat down on the bed beside her. Pregnancy, however, was affecting the stability of her emotions and her mouth trembled as the tears streamed down her face. He put an arm around her. "Sweetheart, don't cry," he begged. "I'm sorry. I didn't mean to upset you." Then, as she only cried harder, "Frances, please stop crying!"

But her head was buried in his shoulder and she was sobbing now in earnest. Once started she couldn't seem to stop. "You yelled at me about my dress!" she wept into his soaked dressing gown.

He was patting her soothingly on the back. "I'm

sorry, I'm sorry," he repeated. "I didn't mean it. It was a beautiful dress. You looked beautiful."

She hiccuped. "You didn't even dance with me."

"I'm sorry," he said again, feeling like a talking parrot who only knew one phrase. The sobs seemed to be slowing and he gently stroked her hair. "Sh, sh, now, mo chridhe. The Condessa is not worth all this grief, believe me." He took a handkerchief out of his pocket and, tipping her face up, carefully dried her eyes, then gave it to her. "Blow," he said. She did and he leaned forward to kiss her forehead. "Now go back to sleep, please. You'll feel better in the morning." He stood up.

"All right," she replied in a watery voice, and lay back again, her hair spilled over the pillow. He pulled the cover over her shoulder, touched her lightly on the cheek, then went quietly back to his own room, shaken himself by the unexpected scene. It was not until he was blowing out the candle that an unnerving thought struck him. She had never answered his question about James Campbell of Ardkinglas.

As the days went by it became increasingly clear to Frances that Margaret was meeting James Campbell outside the shelter of her chaperonage. It was all done so casually—a chance meeting at the library, at the shops, in the park. Only the encounters were planned, and the man and girl were not engaged in careless flirtation. This was the real thing, but it was happening between two people who were separated by a blood enmity that made the quarrel between the Montagues and the Capulets seem trivial. What was worse, Frances was afraid that Ian suspected. There was no mistaking his growing hostility to Campbell. It was all right to join with the Campbells in business, but a marriage between the families would obviously be unthinkable in his eyes. He was displeased with her as well, probably for failing to prevent his sister from enjoying the company of this hereditary enemy.

Frances was caught in the middle. She wanted to please Ian but all her sympathy was with Margaret, whose proud young soul was torn by conflicting emotions. She came in one afternoon to hear Margaret picking out a tune on the piano in the drawing room. She recognized it instantly. It was the Macdonald battle song. She listened as Margaret sang bleakly in Gaelic:

Fallen race of Campbell—disloyal, untrue
No clan in the Highlands will sorrow for you
But the birds of Loch Leven are wheeling on
    high
And Lochaber's wolves hear the Macdonald's cry
'Come feast! Come feast! where the false-
    hearted lie!'

The music stopped, Margaret bowed her head, and Frances said gently. "Would you like to talk about him, Maggie? I'll help you if I can."

Margaret turned to look at her, a desolate look in her dark eyes. "No one can help me, Frances."

"Darling, don't look like that." Frances crossed the room to put comforting arms around her young sister-in-law. "It can't be as bad as that."

"It is. If I marry the man I love I'll become a pariah to my family. And I will never love anyone but Jamie. You may not believe me, but it is true."

"I believe you," Frances said quietly. Something in the quality of her voice pierced through Margaret's self-enclosed misery and she raised her eyes.

"Yes, you would," she answered slowly. "It's always been Ian for you, hasn't it, Frances?"

Frances' head was averted and there was something almost austere in the pure lines of her profile. "Yes," she said.

Margaret's eyes were steady on her. "But you married someone else." Frances turned to face Margaret's dark, searching eyes. There was a look of stretched transparency about her face that Margaret noticed for the first time. She frowned in concern. "Never mind, Frances. I didn't mean to question you."

"It is all right," Frances replied in a contained voice. "Like Othello I was one who loved not wisely but too well. I sent Ian away, an action I came to regret bitterly. I should hate to see you make the same mistake."

"But everything has worked out all right. I mean, you are together now."

"Sometimes, Maggie, you can't undo the past. The Bible tells us that to everything there is a season. If the right season for love is allowed to pass it may prove difficult to recapture at a later time."

"That's not true for you!" Margaret cried.

"I don't know." Frances said tiredly.

There was silence in the room then Margaret asked, "Does Ian suspect about us?"

"I don't know."

"He has become impossible lately. He—he was extremely rude to Jamie yesterday. And Jamie has been so helpful to him about the loan!"

"I know. He used to like Mr. Campbell very much."

181

Margaret's face looked stark. "He must know something. Oh God, Frances, what am I going to do?"

"Give it a little more time, Margaret."

"I'll be eighteen next week," the girl replied. Green eyes met brown in perfect comprehension.

"Yes," said Frances. "It would be so much nicer, though, to have your brother's consent."

"I know. And Mama—how can I do that to her, Frances? She's already lost two sons."

"I'll tell you something, Maggie," Frances said with sudden bitterness. "Love isn't all it is cracked up to be."

"No," replied Margaret in the same tone, "it's much more pleasant in novels."

Meanwhile the cause of all their problems was suffering from the same malady himself. He couldn't be happy with Frances nor could he leave her alone. Nell had returned but her presence did nothing to alleviate the strife that had arisen between him and Frances. He was domineering and autocratic and she resented it. But he could not help himself. The only time he felt she was truly his was when he made love to her. Then all his fears receded and she was once more his own sweet love. But this kind of dual life could not continue.

The evening of her conversation with Margaret, Frances was sitting in bed reading a book when she heard Ian come into the room next door. She frowned. He was supposed to have been dining at Brooks' with Douglas. The door to her room opened and he came in, his face looking dark against the opened collar of his white shirt.

"What are you doing home so early?" she asked.

"I got bored. What about you?"

"I told you I was staying home tonight." She had, and one of the reasons he had come back was to check up on her. He crossed the room and stood beside the bed, regarding her lazily from his height.

"Don't tell me you're bored too? You'll need to acquire a few new admirers to brighten things up. I don't know how you are going to survive when we go home to Lochaber."

Her eyes were like emeralds in her translucent face. "Why are you like this?" she whispered, and clenched her hands together.

"Like what?" he said, deliberately misunderstanding her. "Don't you want to go home to Lochaber, Frances?"

She closed her book and put it down. "What do you want, Ian?" she asked coldly. His eyes narrowed and he took a step closer to her when she said sharply, "No!" His eyes widened in surprise. "You cannot alternately bully me and ignore me by day and expect to come in here and sleep with me at night. You must see that you are making life impossible for me."

"I thought you liked to sleep with me," he said deliberately.

Color stained her cheeks and her voice shook as she replied, "If you get into bed with me, Ian, it will be against my will. I cannot scream and fight you, not with our daughter sleeping two doors down from here. But I want you to leave me alone!"

There was a ruthless look about his mouth. "If I leave here I have somewhere else to go," he said.

"Then go!" she cried passionately.

He turned on his heel and left the room

Chapter Twenty-two

But had I wist, before I kist
  That love had been so ill to win,
I had lock'd my heart in a case o' gowd
  And pinn'd it wi' a siller pin

                —ANONYMOUS

A week after Margaret's conversation with Frances she
and James Campbell met at a ball give by Mrs. Drum-
mond Burrell. He asked her to dance and they waltzed
in silence for some minutes before he said in a stifled
voice, "Margaret, I am going out of my mind. I must
talk to you."

Her black lashes lifted and she shot a fleeting look at
him. He was very pale, his eyes sparkling like blue
diamonds in his set face. Her breath began to come
faster.

"All right," she said.

"We can slip out into the garden. Will you be too
cold?"

She shook her head and he began to circle the dance
floor purposefully until they were by the tall French

doors. With scarcely a break in tempo they moved through the doorway and out into the garden. Frances, on the other side of the room dancing with the Marquis of Bermington, saw them go.

They stood together under the stars and James Campbell of Ardkinglas said fiercely. "I cannot go on like this any longer. I love you, I want to marry you. Let me talk to your brother!"

"He will say no," said Margaret shakily. "You've seen the way he has been acting these past few weeks."

There was a tense silence and then Campbell picked up her long-fingered hand. He kissed it passionately. "Marry me anyway," he said.

"How can I?" Margaret answered brokenly.

He felt so frustrated he wanted to smash his fist into Ian Macdonald's face. "The Campbells are good enough to guarantee his loan for him, but not good enough to marry his sister. Is that it?"

"Jamie!" She flung herself into his arms and he could feel her slender body shaking with sobs. "It isn't just Ian."

He rested his lips against her hair and closed his eyes. He knew that. It was Margaret herself, bound by ties of family and of clan and of loyalties he, who was Highland, perfectly understood. If her brother, the head of her family and her race, gave her permission to marry a Campbell it would make such an action possible. If he did not, their marriage would be a breach of clan loyalty that was almost impossible to one of Margaret Macdonald's upbringing. He could not ask it of her.

"I will talk to him," Campbell said through his teeth. "We have to know. We can't go on like this much longer."

At this the door to the ballroom opened and Frances came out into the garden. She had Douglas with her. James Campbell released Margaret slowly and they turned to face the new arrivals. "I think Margaret should return to the ballroom, Mr. Campbell," Frances said. He looked for a minute into her beautiful, sympathetic eyes and then he nodded.

"Lady Lochaber is right, m'eudail," he said softly to Margaret.

Douglas put a gentle hand on his cousin's arm. "Come along, Maggie. Let me get you something to drink."

She drew herself up to her slim height and nodded. Without looking again at Campbell or Frances she allowed Douglas to lead her back into the ballroom. He procured them both glasses of champagne and found them seats in a little recess off the anteroom. Margaret sipped her wine, then raised her eyes to say something to Douglas and was struck by the look of despair on his face. "Douglas!" she cried. "Is something wrong?"

"No." Then as she continued to look at him in concern he smiled painfully. "I was just remembering a scene very similar to the one just now in the garden."

"What happened?" she asked softly.

"Nothing remarkable. Then it was Ian and Frances who left the ballroom together just as you and Ardkinglas did tonight."

"They slipped out into the garden too?"

Douglas laughed and the sound shocked Margaret. "When did you ever know Ian to do anything surreptitiously? No, he stalked into the ballroom and virtually dragged Frances off the floor with him. I had to go and bring her back, just as we came to fetch you tonight."

"Oh."

He turned to look at her. "Do you love that young man, Maggie?"

"Yes. I love that young man."

"Why, then, does he not ask for you?"

"He wants to. He will. But I don't think Ian will give his consent." She was staring down into her lap. "He has changed. There is something wrong between him and Frances. I don't know what it is but Frances is deeply unhappy. She doesn't say anything but one can tell."

"I know," he answered bleakly.

"He is seeing that ridiculous Condessa," Margaret said furiously. "How can he be so stupid? You would think that any man lucky enough to have Frances . . ." She broke off as Douglas raised a hand briefly to his eyes. "Douglas!" There was an appalled silence as Margaret stared at his shielded face. She swallowed. "You love her, don't you?"

He didn't answer for a long time, and when he did his voice sounded perfectly normal. "Forever, it seems."

She reached out to cover his hand. "I'm sorry. I didn't know." There was a pause and then she asked directly, "Does she?"

He shooked his head. "You have seen it. Your mother has seen it. But Frances—she has never really noticed any other man but Ian. I don't think it has ever occurred to her that the rest of us are flesh and blood."

"What about Robert Sedburgh?"

"Perhaps Robert Sedburgh. She could not fail to notice him. But she never looked at him the way I have seen her look at Ian."

"Well, the looks she is giving Ian these days are

hardly loving,'' Margaret said bracingly. "And I don't blame her. He is behaving atrociously.''

"Something is bothering him. Let me talk to him, Maggie. Perhaps I can help.''

She smiled at him. "If Ian will listen to anyone it will be to you, Douglas. Thank you.''

Frances and James Campbell remained in the garden for a few minutes after Margaret and Douglas left, and then they returned together to the ballroom. They stood for a moment inside the door, and Campbell bent his head to say something to her. In response she smiled and briefly placed a comforting hand on his arm. A shadow loomed over them and they both looked up to see Ian's great height standing between them and the rest of the room. His black brows were drawn together, his dark face looked distinctly menacing. "Where were you?'' he demanded of Frances.

She raised her chin. "In the garden,'' she responded coolly. "It was stuffy in here and Mr. Campbell kindly escorted me out to get some air.''

He put a hand on her arm and her eyes, long and very green under dark lashes, met his steadily. There was a warning in those eyes, clear to Ian and to the watching Campbell. Do not touch me, they said. *Noli me tangere.* Deliberately he slid his hand down her arm and then raised her hand to his lips. He turned to look at James Campbell, such open hostility on his face that Campbell involuntarily stepped back a pace. Murder was looking at him out of Ian Macdonald's eyes and Campbell, dimly, began to perceive what it was that was wrong with the Earl of Lochaber. "But where is the Condessa?''

Frances said. "You musn't let us keep you from her side, Ian."

His eyes were coal black and dangerously narrow as they moved from James Campbell back to Frances. The two pairs of eyes met and locked and Frances suddenly shivered. Her nails drove into the palms of her hands but she refused to turn away from the challenge she read in his look. "I'll see you later," he said softly and turned away leaving her alone with James Campbell by the window.

Frances began to shake, and James Campbell considerately moved to shield her from the eyes of the rest of the room. Ian had left the ballroom, walking past the Condessa as if he had not seen her. As, indeed, he hadn't. "Are you all right, Lady Lochaber?" Campbell asked in concern. He was shaken himself by the intense unspoken emotions of that brief scene he had just witnessed. He could not understand how Lochaber could behave so brutally to his serenely beautiful and gentle wife.

With heroic effort Frances forced down her rising temper. She schooled her face to an expression of aloof reserve and looked at James Campbell. "I am perfectly fine, Mr. Campbell," she said evenly. But she could not disguise her eyes and Campbell, looking at their brilliant, glittering green, experienced another shock. Panther's eyes, Douglas had called them, and it was a description James Campbell would have agreed with. He thought, suddenly, that he would not like to cross swords with Frances Macdonald. Unexpectedly he felt a flicker of sympathy for Ian.

*   *   *

Ian walked right past Margaret and Douglas without seeing them either. 'Dhé!'' said Margaret. ''What is wrong with Ian?''

''I don't know, Maggie,'' returned Douglas. ''I think we ought to find Frances, though. She is the only person with the power to make him look like that.''

Frances, however, was uncommunicative when asked about Ian. ''Perhaps he had an argument with the Condessa,'' she said dulcetly. And only for an instant had the daggers shown in her cool green eyes.

Chapter Twenty-three

The long love that in my thought doth harbour,
And in mine heart doth keep his residence,
—SIR THOMAS WYATT

Frances stayed at the ball until almost two in the morning. She was silent in the carriage on the way home, but she had been more silent than usual these past few weeks, so Margaret was not unduly worried. She herself was not in the mood for chatter.

Ian had not yet arrived home. When she received this information from the night footman Frances merely nodded. Ian had not been home until early morning all this week and she knew it. She knew, also, where he was. The fact that she herself had sent him there did not make her blame him any the less. All week she had treated him with gentle, cold courtesy, shutting him out as effectively as if he had been a stranger with whom she had no desire to become better acquainted. He had not tried to come near her again. But tonight. . . . She remembered his words and for the first time in their marriage she locked the connecting door between their rooms.

She was very tired, worn out with nerves and pregnancy and the lateness of the hour. She closed her eyes while her maid brushed her hair and only opened them when the woman lifted the heavy, palely gleaming mass to plait it. "Leave it, Mary," she said wearily. "I'm too tired to sit here any longer."

"Very well, my lady," Mary answered obediently. She took the rich velvet robe that Frances handed her and watched as her mistress, clad only in a thin white hand-embroidered nightgown got into bed. "Goodnight, my lady," she said then.

"Goodnight, Mary," Frances said sleepily. As the door closed behind the maid Frances snuggled down under the covers. In ten minutes she was asleep.

Ian came home at three. He had gone to Brooks' after leaving the ball and the intervening time he had spent drinking. Drinking and thinking of Frances. By the time he reached Mount Street he was in a savage mood. He went upstairs to his bedroom, allowed his valet to help him off with his coat, and then suddenly dismissed him. He waited until the man had gone down the hall before he moved with decision to the door that connected his room to Frances's.

It was locked.

For a stunned moment Ian didn't realize what was the matter. Impatiently he rattled the knob, but nothing happened. Slowly it dawned on him. *She had locked him out.*

White-hot temper seared through his veins. He put his shoulder against the door, testing. Then, with three strong thrusts that sounded thunderous in the quiet of the sleeping house, he forced the door open.

Frances was sitting up in bed, the covers pulled up to

her chin, her wide eyes fixed on the door. "What do you think you are doing?" she asked in a low, trembling voice.

He was standing in front of the open door, a candle in his hand. With his free hand he reached behind him to close the door. It crashed, shuddering, into its frame and he walked a few more paces into the room, his eyes on his wife. He held the candle up so he could see her better and then said softly, "Come here."

Suddenly Frances was afraid. She had never seen him this angry before, and the fact that his voice had been carefully controlled only made him seem more dangerous. "Ian," she said. "Please . . ."

He put the candle down carefully. She could see that his fists were clenched. Her heart was hammering. "I said 'come here,' " he said again in that same frighteningly level tone.

Slowly she got out of bed until she stood, barefoot, on the cold floor. He didn't move and she came across the room to stand before him, her eyes enormous in her pale face. She was afraid of what he was going to do and said the only thing she could think of to stop him. "Ian. Please. I'm going to have a baby."

His head rocked back a little as if she had struck him. He stared at her as if she were a stranger. The candle threw its light upward, illuminating the planes and angles of her beautiful face. She was tearing him apart and he wanted to hurt her. "Oh?" he said finally, in a cold, galling voice. "And whose is this one?"

There was a stunned silence then Frances suddenly whirled and, picking up a thin china vase that stood on a table beside her, struck out at him furiously "I hate you!" she cried.

He raised his arm instinctively to protect himself and the vase crashed against it, smashing before it even hit the floor. Blood stained the white lawn of his shirt sleeve. He heard the sharp intake of her breath but, curiously, the pain had served to clear his own head. Without looking at her he rolled his sleeve up exposing his hard forearm, brown and strong and torn now with an ugly red gash. He took his handkerchief from his pocket and handed it to Frances. "Tie it up for me," he said in a voice that was almost normal.

She had been staring at his arm with huge, dilated eyes. Now she took his handkerchief and with shaking hands bound it tightly around the wound. She was standing very close to him and when she had finished she tipped her head back to look up at him. His arms went around her and he bent his head. Their mouths met with a passionate violence that shocked them both. He lifted her in his embrace so that her feet were off the floor. She could feel the powerful muscles of his back under her hands. Then she was lying on the bed. His deep voice, murmuring in Gaelic, was in her ears. She clung to him, wanting him to take her, moving with him in violent intensity.

He had wanted to hurt her. When he had broken into her room rape had been on his mind. But it was not just her revelation about the baby that had defused his hostility. With the feel of her under his hands, the sweetness of her mouth under his, it was impossible to think of anything except his love of her, his need of her. The unexpected wildness of her response released all his own brakes. But behind the almost brutal power of his passion there was, unmistakably, love.

* * *

Frances lay still, feeling the weight of his body as it lay halfway across hers. Her eyes opened slowly to find his dark gaze fixed on her face. She felt herself smiling at him. "I'm sorry about your arm," she said in a husky voice.

"Frances." She was incredibly beautiful as she lay there, her pale hair loose on the pillow. She bent her head to kiss his shoulder.

"I adore you," she said. Her eyes between the long lashes were misty green and tender.

He couldn't believe her. Not even after what had just passed between them. Pain knifed through him as he remembered how she had smiled at James Campbell. Had she ever said to Robert Sedburgh, "I adore you?" He couldn't ask her. He thought, suddenly, that she had got her way again. Well, if she thought he was going to be her willing slave she was mistaken. He rolled over onto his elbow and looked at her with now inscrutable eyes. "Your lovers have taught you well," he drawled with calculated brutality.

Frances stared at him incredulously. The sudden change in him from passionate lover to cold accuser bewildered her. "What did you say?" she asked faintly.

He merely shrugged and, getting out of bed, began to dress. His actions even more than his words penetrated her dazed mind. He was leaving her. After what she had just done with him, he was leaving her. She felt numbed and betrayed.

Her silence affected him as her anger would not have. He tucked his shirt into his pants and turned to look at her. "You are my wife," he said. "Don't ever lock your door to me again."

Was that what it was all about, she thought confusedly. An assertion of his rights? He stood there before her, arrogant, domineering, cruel, the man who only fifteen minutes ago had been saying such things to her, doing such things to her. The first drops of bitter gall began to well up in her heart. "You bastard." Her voice was taut and very low.

He laughed. "You should know about bastards, sweetheart."

Frances was shaking with passion as she answered "I will never forgive you for this, Ian."

He shrugged his big shoulders in seeming indifference. "Don't lock that door again," he repeated and walked with lazy grace to the door in question and opened it. He hesitated for a moment on the threshold then, without looking back, went through to his own room. It closed firmly behind him.

Frances lay back and stared with burning eyes at the canopy over her bed. She stayed thus until the morning light began to filter into the room. Then she resolutely closed her eyes to try to get a few hours sleep. She would need it; she had a great many things to do before evening fell again.

Chapter Twenty-four

We twa hae paidled i' the burn,
    From morning sun till dine;
But seas between us braid hae roared
    Sin' auld lang sayne.

—ROBERT BURNS

Margaret was sitting up in bed the next morning sipping coffee when there came a knock on her door. "Come in," she called and then stared in astonishment as her sister-in-law, dressed in a tan walking dress, came into the room. "Frances!" she said, putting down her coffee. "What are you doing up at this hour?" It was eight o'clock and Frances had not been appearing until at least ten recently.

"I'm terribly sorry to have to do this to you, Margaret," Frances replied, "but I am leaving today for Edinburgh."

"What!"

"Yes. I am taking Nell with me."

"Has something happened? Your father?"

"Papa is fine as far as I know. What has happened is

199

that I am leaving Ian. And I want to be gone before he returns.''

"Dhé," said Margaret. "Is it as bad as all that?"

"Yes." Frances's face was tired and strained looking. but she held her head proudly on her lovely neck and the eyes that looked at Margaret were steady and cool.

"Are you all right, Frances?" Margaret asked anxiously.

"Yes," her sister-in-law said again.

"How do you plan to travel?"

"I'll hire a chaise."

"A chaise! You can't travel to Scotland in a chaise. Not with Nell. Not in your condition." Margaret had realized the cause of Frances's uncharacteristic lassitude about two weeks ago.

"Yes I can," Frances replied stubbornly.

Margaret pushed back the covers and got out of bed. She went over to Frances and put an arm around her. "Darling, what happened?" she asked gently. Frances merely shook her head, her mouth curving into a line of pain. "Never mind," Margaret said hastily. "It doesn't matter. I'm coming with you."

Frances smiled shakily. "Thank you, Maggie, but that's not necessary."

"Yes, it is," replied Margaret uncompromisingly. "What is more, I'll see to the transportation. You get yourself and Nell packed."

"But Maggie," Frances protested in bewilderment.

"Ian is a brute," returned his loving sister. "I certainly don't want to stay here with him. With you gone he'll only take out his bad temper on me." She gave Frances a gentle push. "Go on. I've got to get dressed."

"But what are you going to do?" asked Frances, moving obediently toward the door.

"Send for Jamie," said Margaret. "He'll know the best way for us to travel. Goodbye. I'll see you later." She closed her door behind Frances and then went to ring for her maid.

James Campbell did indeed know the best way for them to travel. The Duke of Argyll's yacht was anchored at Dover. As the Duke was in Ireland and would not be returning for several more weeks Campbell did not hesitate to place it at the service of his beloved. "I'll escort you to Dover and then come back to London. I want to talk to Lochaber about us."

Margaret looked very somber. "Whatever he says, Jamie, it doesn't matter. I'll marry you anyway."

Color stained his fair face. "Do you mean that, m'eudail?"

"Yes." He caught her to him and for a long time neither of them spared a thought for Frances or her dilemma. Then he released her reluctantly. "I'd better go, Margaret. I'll be back in two hours with a chaise and we'll leave for Dover."

"All right. And thank you, Jamie. It is not every man who would help in a situation like this."

He knew that and ordinarily he wouldn't himself dream of helping a wife run away from her husband. But there had been a disturbingly ugly note in that little scene he had witnessed between Frances and Ian last night. In his opinion Frances was better off out of the way until Ian had had a chance to calm down. And, selfishly, he wanted Margaret out of Ian's way as well. At least until he had had a chance to see how Ian reacted to a proposal for the heart and hand of his sister.

Nell was bewildered when Frances told her they were leaving immediately for Scotland. "But why, Mama?" she kept saying. Frances trotted out one lame excuse after the other as she supervised the maid who was packing Nell's clothing. Finally the little girl came over and took a firm hold on her skirt. "Are you and Dada angry?" she asked in a small voice.

Frances looked down into the troubled eyes of her daughter and suddenly knelt beside her. "Yes," she said honestly.

"Why?" asked Nell, her eyes growing larger and more worried.

"It has nothing to do with you, darling," Frances said briskly. "It is a quarrel that is strictly between grownups."

"Oh." Nell rubbed her hand across Frances's arm. "Will Dada be coming to Scotland soon?"

"I don't know," replied Frances flatly.

"Oh," Nell said again. But she obediently packed the toys she wanted to take and asked Frances no more questions. Dada was new and exciting and fun but Mama was the anchor rock of her whole existence. Nell wasn't going to take any chances on being left behind.

They left London at two in the afternoon and by eight o'clock they were in Dover. They boarded the Duke of Argyll's yacht and sailed for Scotland with the ten o'clock tide.

Ian did not return to Mount Street until nine the following morning. His butler met him with the news that Lady Lochaber had departed. She had left him a

note. Ian went into the library and tore open the enve-
lope. There were exactly three sentences for him to
read. "I have gone home to Scotland. Margaret insisted
on coming with me. I have taken Nell. Frances."

Ian was still sitting in the library at one o'clock in the
afternoon when his butler announced the arrival of James
Campbell. "Show him in," Ian said harshly.

James Campbell of Ardkinglas came into the room
and stood regarding the strong profile of the Earl of
Lochaber as he sprawled in a chair staring into the fire.
Suddenly Ian turned and his eyes, black and inimical,
met the steady blue gaze of James Campbell. "What do
you want, Ardkinglas?" he grated. "And what do you
know about my wife?"

"I know that your wife is so upset she felt it necessary
to leave you. And she does not appear to me to be a
woman who is easily upset." Ian slowly rose to his
feet, but Campbell stood his ground. "To answer your
other question," he continued evenly, "I am here to tell
you that I want to marry your sister."

It was a moment before Campbell's words reached
Ian and when they did his eyes widened. "My sister?"
he said. "You want to marry Margaret?"

"I want to marry Margaret. I have wanted to marry
Margaret since first I saw her. I think I may take the
liberty of saying that she also desires to marry me." Ian
said nothing, and Campbell, watching his face, saw
confirmed there what he had begun to suspect the night
of Mrs. Burrell's ball. "You are a fool, Lochaber," he
said roughly. "What have you done?"

"Christ," said Ian, staring at him with appalled eyes.
"You mean it wasn't Frances?"

"Lady Lochaber has been very kind to both Margaret and myself. We were aware, of course, of your growing hostility to me. We all assumed you suspected my feelings for your sister and did not approve."

Ian swore.

"Yes, it seems we have all been dealing at cross purposes," Campbell said pleasantly. "I take it you do not have any great objections to my marrying Margaret?"

"Christ, man, of course not! After the help you've given me, how could I possibly object?"

"Well, you must admit you have hardly been brotherly of late."

Ian ran his hand through his hair. "That was because I thought . . ."

"Yes. I know now what you thought. And I'll tell you again you are a fool. Not for thinking that I—or any man—might fall in love with Lady Lochaber, but for thinking that she might reciprocate."

Ian's formidable face looked suddenly haggard. "Where is she?" he asked.

"I put her on my uncle's yacht at Dover. They are sailing to Leith. Lady Lochaber plans to go to her father in Edinburgh. Margaret is returning to Castle Hunter."

"I'll go after her," Ian said decisively.

"I'm afraid I don't have another boat."

"Dhé. If I go by land it will take me twice as long." Campbell frowned. "True. We need a boat."

"We?"

"*I* am going to Lochaber."

Dark eyes met blue. "Very well," Ian said. "Then let us see about a boat. I'll go talk to my cousin."

"I'll go on to Brooks'. There may be some people there who can help. Meet me there in two hours?"

"Good." Ian moved to the door with restless energy. "Let's get going, Ardkinglas." He paused for a moment and then held out his hand. "I owe you an apology." The other man took his hand and Ian suddenly smiled. Campbell, as helpless as most against the irresistible charm of that look, smiled back. They stood thus for a moment and then broke apart, leaving the room together.

Douglas was working in his studio when Ian called. He came slowly into the comfortable room that served for most of his needs and regarded his cousin's strong, exciting face with a notable lack of enthusiasm. "What is so urgent that you must drag me from my work?" he asked crossly.

"I need a boat to get to Scotland," Ian said baldly. "Do you know anyone who might have one?"

"A boat?" Douglas stared at Ian blankly. "But why?"

Ian's mouth twisted. "I've made a mess of things, Douglas, and Frances has left me. She sailed yesterday on Argyll's yacht. I want to follow her."

"I should say you have made a mess of things if you've driven her to this," Douglas responded grimly. "What devil has gotten into you, Ian, that you must behave so outrageously?"

Ian merely looked bleak and said nothing.

"God! And she is expecting a child as well! You ought to be horsewhipped," Douglas said furiously.

Ian's head came up. "How do you know about the child?"

"I'm an artist. It's my business to observe closely." There was a pause, then Douglas added almost unwillingly, "I am particularly observant where Frances is concerned."

"So I see." Ian's dark eyes were fixed with sudden shrewdness on his cousin's face. "My mother was right, after all, wasn't she, Douglas?" he finally said slowly. Douglas shrugged but Ian continued to regard him wonderingly. "You have always been there, stepping forward again and again to shield her, to help her. I don't know why I never saw it before."

"*She* has never seen it," said Douglas painfully. "Why, then, should you?"

"True," Ian replied bitterly. "I have hardly been seeing clearly these past few weeks. That has now been made abundantly plain to me."

"What happened?" Douglas asked diffidently, and Ian, who had had no intention of confiding in him, decided to tell his cousin the truth. In a confused way he felt he owed it to him.

"I was jealous," he said wearily. "Of Ardkinglas."

"What?!"

"Yes. That was Campbell's reaction as well. It seems all along he has been trying to fix his interest with Maggie. I thought it was Frances. So I blew up and acted the fool, as Ardkinglas so pithily informed me."

"Ian, how could you have been stupid enough to believe that Frances would return Ardkinglas' supposed advances—or anyone else's for that matter?" Douglas was looking at him in amazement.

Ian was by now sprawled in a chair, his eyes firmly fixed on the tips of his boots. "That is what Campbell said."

"Campbell appears to have said a great many sensible things. Good God—Frances. Why even when she is furious with you, as she has been these past weeks, still she has no thought for any man else.''

"She did—once,'' Ian replied in a low tone. He still refused to meet Douglas's eyes.

There was a very long silence. "Ian. Are you jealous of Robert Sedburgh?'' Douglas finally asked quietly. There was no reply and Douglas began to laugh softly. "Poor Frances,'' he said, shaking his head in rueful wonder. "So history repeats itself.''

At that Ian raised his eyes. "What do you mean?''

"I mean that Robert Sedburgh was jealous of you. And with far more reason, I might add.''

A flame flickered in Ian's eyes. "Do you mean that, Douglas?''

"I do.'' Douglas sighed and leaned back in his chair. "She was a good wife to him, I think. I even think she was—content. I don't know. The only one who has ever really penetrated that unruffled serenity Frances presents to the world is you. There may have been love in her for Robert Sedburgh. But not passion. That belongs to only you.'' He removed his eyes from the mantelpiece and looked at Ian. "She waited for you. She could have had anyone but she waited for you. You weren't home three weeks before she married you. How could you have doubted her, Ian?''

"Christ, Douglas, I don't know. It has been eating away at me. Why did she marry him? Why didn't she send for me?''

"She was very, very angry with you.''

"Yes, I suppose she was.'' He rubbed his hands across his eyes. "She is just as angry at me now. And she has a right to be,'' he added honestly.

"What are you going to do?''

"Follow her to Edinburgh and grovel at her feet," Ian said wryly. "Nothing less than that will do, I'm afraid."

Douglas smiled faintly. "Just don't bully her, Ian."

"Bully her!" Ian rose to his intimidating height. "Didn't I just say I planned to grovel?"

"Yes. That is what you said."

Ian stared at him suspiciously for a minute and then moved toward the door. "You don't have a boat at your disposal I take it?"

"No, I do not."

Ian put his hand on the doorknob and his face was surprisingly vulnerable. "What if she won't listen to me, Douglas? She said she would never forgive me."

Douglas bent his head. "I don't think there is anything Frances would not forgive you, Ian. But it seems you are the only one who cannot see that." When he looked up his cousin had gone.

Chapter Twenty-five

Returne the, hairt, hameward agane,
  And byd quhair thou was wont to be
                          —ALEXANDER SCOTT

Ardkinglas had found a boat whose owner was willing to hire it out for a trip to Scotland, so they were only two days behind Frances and Margaret. Their yacht docked at Leith, one of Edinburgh's principal ports, and Ian hired a carriage and drove directly to Lochaber House on the Canongate. Frances was not there. With a somewhat grim look about his mouth, Ian offered a night's hospitality to James Campbell before he set out on the long ride to Castle Hunter. Campbell accepted and was comfortably ensconced in the Macdonald library when Ian left for Frances's father's house in Charlotte Square. Here he had better luck.

"Lord Lochaber!" Sir Donal's butler looked first surprised to see him and then distinctly nervous.

"Is my wife here?" Ian asked uncompromisingly.

"Well—er—yes, my lord. But I do not know if she is in at present."

"I'll just see for myself, thank you," said Ian, and he shouldered his way past the butler and down the hall to the drawing room. He threw open the door and she was there, sitting empty-handed in front of the fireplace. She rose slowly, her hand holding to the back of her chair, as if for support.

"How did you get here?" The knuckles of her hand showed white.

"Ardkinglas found us a boat." Her brows rose at the mention of Campbell's name, but she said nothing. "I must talk to you," he said. "Please, Frances."

There was a brief pause and then she nodded slowly. "That will be all, Weldon, thank you." The butler withdrew from the room, closing the door behind him, and Ian was left facing his wife. Her face was contained. There was nothing in it to tell him what she would say or do after he had spoken. He began slowly. "The last time we met in this room there was five years of separation between us. The gap, now, seems so much wider."

"Yes," she said merely.

He took a deep breath. "Frances. I've come to beg you to forgive me. I don't know what got into me to make me say such things to you." Her face never changed and he continued, in a rush, bitterly, "No, that's not true. I do know what was wrong with me. I was jealous."

"Jealous?" She sounded unbelieving.

"Yes. I thought you were in love with Ardkinglas."

"You thought? . . ." Anger began to sparkle in her eyes. "Were you out of your mind?"

"Yes," he replied somberly. "I rather think I was."

"And what disabused you of this extremely odd notion?" she said coldly.

"Ardkinglas did. He told me he wanted to marry Maggie."

"And what did you say?"

"I said yes, of course," he replied impatiently. "What possible objection could I have to Ardkinglas?"

"Well, you were perfectly beastly to him," she said warmly.

"I know, I know." He ran his hand through his thick hair. "But don't you see, Frances, I thought it was you he was interested in? He seemed to be constantly around you. Everywhere I went I was tripping over him. And you wouldn't tell me why you were suddenly so interested in him, why you spent so much time in conversation with him." His dark eyes were intent on her face. "Men have been falling in love with you for years. You can't blame me for not seeing he was after Maggie."

"You never before suspected *me*," she said carefully.

He paced to the window and back, his long, lion's prowl of a walk making the room seem like a cage. He stopped at the writing desk and stared with interest at the inkwell. "It wasn't just Ardkinglas," he said in such a low voice that she had to strain to hear him.

"I see." She sat back down in her chair. "You had better tell me the whole."

"It is Sedburgh," he said in the same low voice.

She was frowning now, her eyes fixed on his down-looking face. "What do you mean, Ian? Surely you haven't been jealous of Rob?" He didn't answer, but the flicker of a muscle in his cheek betrayed him. "But he has been dead for two years!" she said in astonishment.

"Has he been, Frances? To you?"

"Ian!"

At that he turned to look at her. "Why else won't you let Nell give up his name?" As she stared at him, speechless, he went on doggedly. "Why else did you marry him, Frances?"

The room was filled with an aching silence then Frances said, "I told you why I married him. Because of Nell."

"You should have sent for me," he replied stubbornly.

"Yes." She rose from her chair and went to poke for a minute at the fire. She sat back down again on the sofa and said quite simply, as if very tired, "The truth is, Ian, I married him to spite you."

"What?"

"Yes. It is not something I'm proud of but it is the truth." She met his eyes and her own were full of pain. "I was jealous too. I couldn't forgive you for not putting me first, for needing something else besides me. And so when I found out I was pregnant I took my revenge."

"Frances." He came across the room slowly and dropped down on one knee beside her, his gaze fixed intently on her face. Her eyes looked gray and cloudy.

"You wanted to know why I didn't send for you?" She spoke with bitter truth. "Well that is the reason." She swallowed. "It was the biggest mistake of my life."

"Is that why you wouldn't let me change Nell's name?" he asked gently. "Because you still haven't forgiven me?"

"No!" she cried in distress. "You don't understand."

He sat down beside her on the sofa. "Tell me, then."

"Rob was a wonderful man, Ian," she said in an aching voice. "A strong, gentle, fine man. He loved me. He would have done anything for me. And I had so little left to give him." As he listened to her Ian felt as if the hard, hurting knot that had lodged within him for so long was slowly dissolving. "He deserved so much more than he ever got from me," she was saying. "I couldn't even give him a child." A stab of fierce pride went through him. He had gotten her with child twice. She lifted her face to him and there were tears on it. "That was why I couldn't take Nell from him. He loved her so. She was the only real thing I ever gave him. And even she belongs to you."

He put his arms around her. "Don't cry, mo chridhe. I understand."

"I tried to make him happy," she sobbed into his shoulder.

"Sweetheart, I am so sorry." His lips were in her hair. "I have been so stupid."

She shook her head. "No. It was all my fault. My dreadful temper. I never should have married him. I knew that and I did it anyway."

"Shh. It's all right now."

"Then you came back," she said in muffled tones. "And I was so happy. At Loch Shiel and at Castle Hunter. Then you changed . . ."

"I know." He held her closer. "I'm so sorry. I said such unforgivable things to you. I could tear my tongue out." She merely shook her head and sobbed harder. He loosened his hold on her after a little and said with a hint of amusement in his voice, "I think we've played this scene before. How many more times do you want me to say I'm sorry?"

The sobbing slowed. Finally she said with a watery chuckle, "I always cry a lot when I'm pregnant."

"For nine months?" he said in mock horror.

She laughed and sat up. "No. It's always worse at the beginning." She took the handkerchief he offered and began mopping up. When she had finished she turned to look at him and what she saw on his face made her feel suddenly weak.

"I love you, Frances. There has never been anyone else for me. There never will be. Will you come back to me? We'll put these weeks in London behind us and go back to what we had at Loch Shiel. Can you do that?"

She looked at him with misty eyes. "Oh, Ian. I'll do anything you want. You know that."

His dark face lit with his blazing smile. "The amazing thing, Frances, is that you really believe that."

"Of course I do!" she said indignantly. "What do you mean?" But he shook his head and wouldn't answer.

When Sir Donal came home with Nell his butler informed him quietly that Lord Lochaber had arrived and was in the drawing room with Lady Lochaber. Sir Donal sent Nell upstairs and walked cautiously to the door of the room. He heard Frances crying and put his hand on the doorknob. Then came Ian's voice, deep and gentle with a note in it that Sir Donal had never heard before. He hesitated, then took his hand away and went instead to his library.

Fifteen minutes later Nell came back downstairs and went to the drawing room to look for her mother. She opened the door and stood for a minute in stunned surprise. Ian was sitting in her grandfather's big chair and Frances was on his lap. His lips were next to her ear and he was murmuring to her in Gaelic. Frances looked absolutely beautiful. "Mama!" said Nell. "Why are you sitting on Dada's lap?"

The two adults started at her voice and after a moment Frances said, "It's all right, darling. Dada and I have made up our quarrel." She tried to get up but a strong arm held her down.

"Come join us, sweetheart," said Ian and Nell trotted over and unselfconsciously climbed up on the chair and squeezed herself in beside Frances on Ian's lap.

"This is nice," she said contentedly. "I don't like it when you fight."

"We've decided we don't either," replied Ian gravely. "We're going to try to be better in future."

"If you try your hardest you almost always succeed," said Nell, parroting one of her mother's favorite child-rearing maxims. Frances began to laugh and Nell squirmed around to look at her. "That's what you always say to me, Mama."

"I know, darling" Frances rested her head contentedly against Ian's hard upper arm. "And it's the truth. I promise."

About the Author

Joan Wolf is a native of New York City who presently resides in Milford, Connecticut, with her husband and two young children. She taught high school English in New York for nine years and took up writing when she retired to rear a family. Her previous books, THE COUNTERFEIT MARRIAGE, A KIND OF HONOR, and A LONDON SEASON, are also available in Signet editions.

𝄐

SIGNET Regency Romances You'll Enjoy

☐ **THE INNOCENT DECEIVER** by Vanessa Gray.
(#E9463—$1.75)*
☐ **THE LONELY EARL** by Vanessa Gray. (#E7922—$1.75)
☐ **THE MASKED HEIRESS** by Vanessa Gray. (#E9331—$1.75)
☐ **THE DUTIFUL DAUGHTER** by Vanessa Gray.
(#E9017—$1.75)*
☐ **THE WICKED GUARDIAN** by Vanessa Gray. (#E8390 $1.75)
☐ **THE WAYWARD GOVERNESS** by Vanessa Gray.
(#E8696—$1.75)*
☐ **THE GOLDEN SONG BIRD** by Sheila Walsh. (#E8155—$1.75)†
☐ **LORD GILMORE'S BRIDE** by Sheila Walsh. (#E8600—$1.75)*
☐ **THE SERGEANT MAJOR'S DAUGHTER** by Sheila Walsh.
(#E8220—$1.75)
☐ **THE INCOMPARABLE MISS BRADY** by Sheila Walsh.
(#E9245—$1.75)*
☐ **MADALENA** by Sheila Walsh. (#E9332—$1.75)
☐ **THE REBEL BRIDE** by Catherine Coulter. (#J9630—$1.95)
☐ **THE AUTUMN COUNTESS** by Catherine Coulter.
(#AE1445—$2.25)
☐ **LORD DEVERILL'S HEIR** by Catherine Coulter.
(#E9200—$1.75)*
☐ **LORD RIVINGTON'S LADY** by Eileen Jackson.
(#E9408—$1.75)*
☐ **BORROWED PLUMES** by Roseleen Milne. (#E8113—$1.75)†

*Price slightly higher in Canada
†Not available in Canada

Buy them at your local

bookstore or use coupon

on next page for ordering.

Ø

Recommended Regency Romances from SIGNET

☐	**ALLEGRA by Clare Darcy.**	(#J9611—$1.95)
☐	**CRESSIDA by Clare Darcy.**	(#E8287—$1.75)*
☐	**ELYZA by Clare Darcy.**	(#E7540—$1.75)
☐	**EUGENIA by Clare Darcy.**	(#E8081—$1.75)
☐	**GWENDOLEN by Clare Darcy.**	(#J8847—$1.95)*
☐	**LADY PAMELA by Clare Darcy.**	(#E9900—$2.25)
☐	**LYDIA by Clare Darcy.**	(#E8272—$1.75)
☐	**REGINA by Clare Darcy.**	(#E7878—$1.75)
☐	**ROLANDE by Clare Darcy.**	(#J8552—$1.95)
☐	**VICTOIRE by Clare Darcy.**	(#E7845—$1.75)
☐	**THE MONTAGUE SCANDAL by Judith Harkness.**	
		(#E8922—$1.75)*
☐	**THE ADMIRAL'S DAUGHTER by Judith Harkness.**	
		(#E9161—$1.75)*
☐	**MALLY by Sandra Heath.**	(#E9342—$1.75)*
☐	**THE COUNTERFEIT MARRIAGE by Joan Wolf.**	
		(#E9064—$1.75)*
☐	**A KIND OF HONOR by Joan Wolf.**	(#E9296—$1.75)*

*Price slightly higher in Canada

Buy them at your local bookstore or use this convenient coupon for ordering.

THE NEW AMERICAN LIBRARY, INC.,
P.O. Box 999, Bergenfield, New Jersey 07621

Please send me the books I have checked above. I am enclosing $_____
(please add $1.00 to this order to cover postage and handling). Send check
or money order—no cash or C.O.D.'s. Prices and numbers are subject to change
without notice.

Name_____

Address_____

City _____ State _____ Zip Code _____
Allow 4-6 weeks for delivery.
This offer is subject to withdrawal without notice.

Ⓢ

Big Bestsellers from SIGNET

☐ **ELISE** by Sara Reavin. (#E9483—$2.95)
☐ **TAMARA** by Elinor Jones. (#E9450—$2.75)*
☐ **LUCETTA** by Elinor Jones. (#E8698—$2.25)*
☐ **BY OUR BEGINNINGS** by Jean Stubbs. (#E9449—$2.50)
☐ **COVENT GARDEN** by Claire Rayner. (#E9301—$2.25)
☐ **SELENA** by Ernest Brawley. (#E9242—$2.75)*
☐ **ALEXA** by Maggie Osborne. (#E9244—$2.25)*
☐ **OAKHURST** by Walter Reed Johnson. (#J7874—$1.95)
☐ **MISTRESS OF OAKHURST** by Walter Reed Johnson.
(#J8253—$1.95)
☐ **LION OF OAKHURST** by Walter Reed Johnson.
(#J8844—$2.25)*
☐ **FIRES OF OAKHURST** by Walter Reed Johnson.
(#E9406—$2.50)
☐ **ABIGAIL** by Malcolm Macdonald. (#E9404—$2.95)
☐ **ECSTASY'S EMPIRE** by Gimone Hall. (#E9242—$2.75)
☐ **LAND OF GOLDEN MOUNTAINS** by Gillian Stone.
(#E9344—$2.50)*
☐ **CALL THE DARKNESS LIGHT** by Nancy Zaroulis.
(#E9291—$2.95)

*Price slightly higher in Canada

Buy them at your local

bookstore or use coupon

on next page for ordering.

Ø

A World of Romance from SIGNET

☐ **PORTRAIT OF LOVE by Lynna Cooper.** (#E9495—$1.75)*
☐ **HEARTS IN THE HIGHLANDS by Lynna Cooper.**
    (#E9314—$1.75)
☐ **FROM PARIS WITH LOVE by Lynna Cooper.** (#E9128—$1.75)*
☐ **SIGNET DOUBLE ROMANCE—HER HEART'S DESIRE by Lynna Cooper and AN OFFER OF MARRIAGE by Lynna Cooper.**
    (#E9081—$1.75)*
☐ **FORGOTTEN LOVE by Lynna Cooper.** (#E8569—$1.75)
☐ **HER HEART'S DESIRE by Lynna Cooper.** (#W8454—$1.50)
☐ **MY TREASURE, MY LOVE by Lynna Cooper.** (#W7936—$1.50)
☐ **AN OFFER OF MARRIAGE by Lynna Cooper.** (#W8457—$1.50)
☐ **SUBSTITUTE BRIDE by Lynna Cooper.** (#W8458—$1.50)
☐ **ALOHA TO LOVE by Mary Ann Taylor.** (#E8765—$1.75)*
☐ **HAWAIIAN INTERLUDE by Mary Ann Taylor.** (#E9031—$1.75)
☐ **LOVER'S REUNION by Arlene Hale.** (#W7771—$1.50)
☐ **STORMY SEA OF LOVE by Arlene Hale.** (#W7938—$1.50)
☐ **THE MOON IN ECLIPSE by Claudia Slack.** (#W8132—$1.50)

*Price slightly higher in Canada

Buy them at your local bookstore or use this convenient coupon for ordering.

THE NEW AMERICAN LIBRARY, INC.,
P.O. Box 999, Bergenfield, New Jersey 07621

Please send me the books I have checked above. I am enclosing $_____
(please add $1.00 to this order to cover postage and handling). Send check or money order—no cash or C.O.D.'s. Prices and numbers are subject to change without notice.

Name_____

Address_____

City _____ State _____ Zip Code _____
Allow 4-6 weeks for delivery.
This offer is subject to withdrawal without notice.